STONE FREE

A STONE COLD THRILLER

J. D. WESTON

WESTON MEDIA

STONE FREE

CHAPTER ONE

When Angie Turvey turned on the lights and laid eyes on her dead neighbour, who hung from Angie's living room wall with six-inch nails through her wrists and ankles, she knew her life was about to change forever.

Emirates flight EK5110 landed at Dubai International Airport at twelve thirty in the morning. Among the business class passengers were Angie Turvey and her eight-year-old daughter, Anya. Angie held her daughter close as they made their way past the flight crew and onto the gangway. She pulled her Louis Vuitton carry-on case behind her, and her daughter pulled her own small bag beside her. The girl's little, pink carry-on contained only a stuffed dog that resembled her own Yorkshire Terrier in London, some colouring books and pens, plus a photo of her with Mickey Mouse and her mum and dad at Disney World. The photo was in a small, wooden frame with the cartoon mouse on the top right corner. Her father had placed it in there without her knowing to keep beside her bed in the family's Dubai villa. He wanted to remind his daughter that he wasn't far away, and even though he couldn't join them on this particular trip, he was thinking of them both.

The chauffeur-driven limousine doors locked automatically with a reassuring, soft click as the car began to move, and the child lay her head on her mother's lap to sleep.

"No, baby, we need to get home," said Angie. "If you sleep now, I'll have to carry you, and I have the cases to carry too."

"I will help you, ma'am," said the driver, with a glance in his rear-view mirror.

"Thank you, sir, but that won't be necessary." She nudged her daughter. "Why don't you tell me what we're going to do on our first day of our holiday, Anya? We're nearly home."

"Tomorrow?"

"Yes, what would you like to do first?"

"Can we play in the sea?"

"Of course we can. Maybe we can have pancakes and then lay on the beach for a while. Would you like that?"

Anya nodded. "Can we also play in the swimming pool?"

The mother took a sharp breath in. "You want to play in the pool, and the sea?"

Anya nodded and gave a little giggle. "Yes, and I want juice with ice."

"Please?"

"Please."

"That's better. I asked Julie to stop by and drop off some basics, so we should be able to make breakfast. But we'll need to go shopping at some point, okay?"

"Shopping?"

"Yes, Anya, we need to buy food for the holiday."

"Okay, but after swimming?"

"Of course. We'll have a nice morning then we'll go buy some food, and if you're a good girl, you know what I'll get you?"

"What, Mummy?"

"Ice-cream."

The girl beamed up at her mum and looked out of the car window.

"But you have to stay awake for another ten minutes, okay?"

"Okay, Mummy."

The Mercedes pulled up outside the villa on frond H of Dubai's prestigious Palm Jumeirah. There was a double garage which contained two cars, a blue Porsche that Angie's husband drove when he was in Dubai, and a larger BMW SUV that was big enough for the whole family, plus shopping and luggage.

"There we go, that wasn't so bad was it?" said Angie as she opened her door. "You'll be in bed in just a few minutes."

The driver walked to the rear of the vehicle to extract the cases, while the mother helped her daughter from the car. She tipped the driver one hundred dirhams and watched as he pulled away. The street was quiet. Each frond of the man-made, palm-shaped island had security at the entrance. The security guards allowed only residents and named guests to enter. The tight security had been one of the features that swayed her and her husband to take the villa. It also limited the amount of traffic on the narrow roads.

There were only fifty villas on each frond, and most of their neighbours were never around. Julie, who lived in the house next door was the only nearby permanent resident. The house on the other side of the Turvey house was rented to holidaymakers, and during the cooler winter months, had a variety of people coming and going.

The mother dragged the large case and the smaller carry-on, while her daughter pulled her own little bag to the front entrance. The large wooden door swung open, and she noticed that Julie had left the lights and the air-conditioning on for her. She made a mental note to thank her for the gesture.

She closed the door behind her and put the cases down.

"Right then, Anya, how about you get off to bed? Do you want me to come and tuck you in?"

Anya nodded and pulled her stuffed dog from the little carry-on.

"Okay, well go get changed, and I'll be up in a sec, okay?"

"On my own?"

"You want me to come with you?"

"It's dark up there."

"Okay, well come on then. I'll come and turn the lights on, but you have to go straight to bed, okay?"

She settled Anya into bed and stroked her hair until she fell asleep then closed the bedroom door behind her and walked down the stairs, hoping that Julie had left a bottle of wine in the fridge.

The stairwell took her back down to the large hallway where her cases were. She left them there and walked towards the rear of the house to the kitchen, which was halfway along the hallway on the right-hand side. She found a bottle of Pinot Grigio in the fridge, silently thanked Julie, and poured herself a glass.

The housekeeper had been recently and cleaned the kitchen, so she relaxed, leaned against the hidden fridge, and took a long tired glance around the immaculate kitchen with its Carrara marble surfaces, and top of the range appliances. They'd done very well. Her husband had taken promotion after promotion, and they had been able to afford a modestly luxurious lifestyle. But she smiled at the fact that she still preferred to drink cheap wine from her crystal glasses.

She shoved off and walked out into the hallway, turning right into the huge lounge and dining area at the very back of the huge, five-bedroom villa.

Angie kicked off her designer boots and reached for the light switches on the wall to her right.

The first switch lit the chandelier above the twelve-seater, lignum vitae dining table in the dining area to her left. The second switch powered the ceiling-mounted spots that were spaced equidistantly around the edge of the room, and on one wall lit the large, three-metre square oil painting by contemporary artist Leonid Afremov.

On the opposite side of the living room, the spots lit the naked and broken body of Julie.

Her head hung limply, and her wide eyes stared as if she'd died in fright. But the blood all over her skin, and the bruises on her face told Angie that Julie had put up a hard fight, and lost. She'd either bled to death or died from internal injuries.

The crystal glass smashed on the tiled floor.

Anya suddenly began to scream from her room.

Then from behind Angie came a chilling, gravelly voice.

"Welcome home, Mrs Turvey."

CHAPTER TWO

Harvey Stone woke at his usual five am, in his usual naked manner, and climbed out of bed onto the ancient hardwood floor before stepping into the en-suite.

The old farmhouse, built in the typical French manner using a tasteful blend of stone and timber for the structure with a slate gabled roof, offered little protection against the brisk winter air outside. There was no double-glazing, and most of the doors were ill-fitting wooden panels that swelled with the summer humidity and shrank to allow the draughts through in the much cooler winter months. But Harvey loved the house. It was everything he needed and nearly everything he owned.

He padded to the kitchen to be greeted by his dog, Boon, then stoked last night's embers in the wood burner. He added a few logs and some kindling then set about putting the kettle on to boil. He found his shorts on the couch and slipped them on; they had been pulled off the previous night when things between Melody and him had gotten lively, and they'd moved their sins to the bedroom.

Harvey leaned against the kitchen worktop, which was wooden and polished to a smooth finish that was flawed only by the century of use it had seen. The old farmhouse still had some work to be done, and although each morning he surveyed the interior, he knew his efforts were needed on the exterior; work on the interior was for the summer. Until then, the roof needed fixing, and gaping holes in the rotting window frames needed caulking. Harvey wasn't really a handyman, but he'd been retired for six months and found the work filled his day nicely.

The kettle started to boil and began its low warning whistle. Harvey took it off the stove and poured the water into the French press. He gave the coffee a minute then added it to the waiting tray and walked back to the bedroom with Boon at his heels.

Melody lay on her side facing the window. The thick duvet clung to her hip, and her naked back welcomed Harvey. He set the tray down on the dresser beside the window and poured coffee into the two mugs. He added fresh cream to Melody's coffee and left his own black.

"There's my man," said Melody. "You made coffee already?"

"You were sleeping."

"Coffee can wait. Why don't you come back to bed?"

"I'm going for a run," said Harvey, and Boon's ears pricked up.

Melody raised herself up onto an elbow to take the mug of coffee from Harvey. "One day, I'm going to teach you how to use long sentences." She smiled up at him as he reached down to kiss her.

"One day, I'm going to teach you that I can't be changed."

"Made of stone, right?"

"Something like that," replied Harvey.

He pulled on a t-shirt, socks and his running shoes while Melody read the news on her phone.

"What's the plan for today then, mister retired man?" asked Melody, looking up at him from inside the covers.

"Windows and maybe see about getting someone in to sort the roof out."

"Don't you want to come to town with me?"

He stepped across the room to her, bent and kissed her on the forehead. "I'll see you later."

"Is that a yes or a no?"

Harvey didn't reply.

He glanced around the house, pulled the front door closed behind him, and checked it was locked. Then Harvey jogged the two hundred yards from the door and along the muddy driveway to the lane that connected the small farmhouse to the beach road at one end and the town of Argeles-Sur-Mer at the other. He sped up to his usual pace and settled into his breathing rhythm. The lane was quiet and dark, and soon the horizon showed the pale, misty blues of the morning Mediterranean.

The only other movement was Boon, who ran in the fields alongside him. A few cars passed sporadically, and each time, Harvey moved from the lane's hard tarmac surface to the rough, bumpy grass hillock to the side. The cars were locals judging by the plates, but the third car had UK plates. It wasn't unusual as tourists often ventured to Argeles-Sur-Mer as a reprise from the less tranquil Riviera further east.

He reached the beach and ran through the long, wild grass that grew on the edge onto the soft, clean sand that led down to the sea. Harvey ran every morning, and each morning he ran a different route; it was an old habit he'd been taught by his mentor Julios to avoid people planning an attack. Many of the routes he took across fields, through the town or through the nearby forests found their way onto the beach eventually, usually as a last sprint before he headed home. Each time he ran on the beach, he'd see the same old guy, stripped down to nothing and swimming in the ocean, no matter the temperature.

"You are early this morning," the man called, holding his hand up in a wave, completely unabashed by his nudity.

Harvey nodded as he passed, and lifted his hand to acknowledge him, and then put his head down and pushed himself harder. He didn't plan his route, he just ran where his legs took him and avoided the places he'd run recently. Harvey turned off the beach before he came to a small village and headed into the fields opposite. As he crossed the road, he caught sight of the small, blue saloon with UK plates. It was parked outside the coffee shop that he and Melody used. Harvey bounded across the field and into the wild forest that lay behind.

An hour later, he turned into the driveway to his farm and slowed to a walk with Boon at his heels. Melody stood in the kitchen clutching a fresh coffee when he opened the back door and they walked back inside.

"Hey, you want more coffee?" asked Melody, reaching down to pat Boon.

"No, I'll take a shower, and get started outside." He headed out of the kitchen.

"Erm, Harvey?"

He stopped and turned to look at Melody.

"Aren't you forgetting something?"

"No, I rarely forget anything."

"My kiss?"

Harvey smiled and stepped across the terracotta-tiled floor, then landed a kiss on her lips.

"You're all sweaty," Melody said. "I *like* it."

"Are you wearing that today?" asked Harvey.

"What?" said Melody, looking down at the loose-knit sweater and jeans. "What's wrong with this?"

"You're going to get dirty."

"Dirty? How?"

"Outside helping me."

"Who said anything about helping you? I'm going into town."

"Oh right. Are you going to walk there in those shoes?"

"Walk? No. I'll take the car."

"Is that right?"

"Yes," said Melody.

"Okay then," said Harvey as he left the room pulling his shirt off.

"Harvey?" called Melody, as he turned the shower on to let the hot water pull through.

"What?"

"Where are the car keys?"

Harvey didn't reply. He smiled to himself, stepped into the shower, and let the hot water run over him.

"Harvey?" Melody was at the bathroom door, leaning against the door frame. He looked up at her. "Did you hear me?"

Harvey switched the water off and ran his hands through his short hair.

"Hand me a towel."

"Where are the keys?"

"Hand me a towel." Harvey broke into a smile.

Melody reached in and took the towel from its hook on the wall. "Where are the keys?"

"Towel."

After a long pause, Melody said, "Keys."

Harvey stepped from the shower cubicle. Melody took a step backwards.

"Give me what *I* want," he said.

"Give me what I want."

"You want keys?"

"Among other things," replied Melody with a smirk.

Harvey walked slowly toward her, as she stepped slowly backwards into the bedroom. The backs of her legs found the bed, and she let herself fall onto the duvet. Harvey strode up to her and looked down. But a movement caught his eye, and he froze. At the far end of the driveway, parked on the lane, was the blue saloon he'd seen twice already that morning. Harvey moved away from the window.

"Stay down."

"What?" said Melody, confused. "What's wrong?"

Harvey began to dress in cargo pants, boots, and a fresh t-shirt, keeping an eye on the car with frequent glances out the window.

"Who's there?" said Melody.

"That's the third time I've seen that car today."

"So what? Probably just tourists."

"UK plate."

"*So?* Tourists," replied Melody.

"No, it doesn't sit right."

"So is the fun over?"

"Get your rifle on them," he said. "I'm going out there."

Harvey slammed the door closed and stepped out onto the muddy driveway. He strode directly down the centre of the track, his eyes fixed on the shape of the driver behind the driver side window. Two more shapes moved in the back totalling three people in the car. He reached within fifty yards of the car when it suddenly pulled away and headed off in the direction of the beach.

Harvey stopped and watched it drive away. He turned back to Melody who was at the bedroom window waving him back.

"You see that?" asked Harvey as he stepped back inside.

"I saw a car with three people in."

"Parked outside our house in the middle of nowhere."

"They're probably lost," said Melody.

"Lost? There's nothing to find."

"Maybe they're looking for somewhere to camp."

"They weren't campers, Melody."

"Ah, forget about them, Harvey," said Melody. "Let's enjoy the day."

"And if they come back?"

"If they come back..." She stepped up close to him and pulled his face down to hers by his shirt. "I'll set my man on them." She kissed him hard on the lips.

Harvey responded by kissing her back briefly then pulling away. "What did you have in mind?"

"In mind?" she said.

"You said you wanted fun. What do you want to do?"

"Oh, why don't we start with breakfast?"

"I could eat," said Harvey. "Where?"

"Why don't we go to the little cafe in the village by the beach?" replied Melody. "I feel like I need something fruity."

"Something fruity, yeah?" said Harvey.

"Mmm," replied Melody, licking her lips seductively.

Harvey saw through the charade. He saw where she was taking the conversation. "First, we train then we eat."

Melody's arms flopped to her sides as Harvey stepped away, and he smiled to himself when he heard her sigh behind him. He whistled for Boon who came running in from where he'd been sleeping on the spare bed.

Their mornings typically involved training of some description. Some mornings they sparred in their barn, where Harvey had set up a few floor mats. Other mornings, they ran together and worked out. Harvey usually led the training, but Melody had recently been teaching him how to shoot a rifle. She had explained to him that a handgun, like the SIG Sauer P226 they had used when they worked together, was not effective at long range, and the automatic MP5s they had used were barbaric and unwieldy in comparison to the skill required to tame a 7.62 sniper rifle. Long range shooting required elegance, practice and precision, and the Diemaco rifle she preferred was the perfect partner for a sniper.

"Let's go, boy," said Harvey, as the dog skipped around in two tight circles by his feet.

Melody pulled on a tight and short leather biker jacket and took the rifle from the gun cabinet in the hallway. "Right, boys, let's go."

The three stepped out into the large field at the rear of the house. Three bales of hay marked the firing position, and a wall of hay, exactly one thousand metres away, marked the target.

Melody had trained at Bisley, one the UK's finest shooting grounds, where volunteers would wait in a bunker below the target, ready to pull the target down, call the shots, and paste a new target on. But in Harvey and Melody's field, they didn't have that luxury. They simply replaced the targets after finishing the session, so a new target was ready whenever they felt the urge to shoot.

Long-range target shooting was Melody's speciality, and for Harvey, there could be no better tutor. She slapped his hand if he gripped the rifle stock, and would tell him to let the rifle lay on his open hand. If he snatched a shot, she wouldn't even call it from the scope, she would simply tut.

Harvey had learned a lot, and as he dropped to the prone position, Melody didn't utter a word to help him. He lay down and got comfortable. The rifle lay across his open left palm and the butt was pulled in tight to his shoulder, finding the sweet spot to absorb the massive kickback from the rifle.

Before he even lowered his head and found the target through the scope, Harvey calmed his breathing. He placed the box of rounds beside him so that he could reload without drop-ping the rifle.

"Groups of five at five inches, five shots in the head, five in the chest," said Melody. "Take your time. How's the wind?"

"Two knots, maybe three," replied Harvey.

"So, what are you going to do?"

"Take a test shot and see where it goes?"

"Negative, Stone," said Melody playfully. "You have a live shooter situation. He has fifty people pinned down and you're their only chance of escaping. What are you going to do?"

Harvey closed his eyes and felt the tiny clicks of the scope as he adjusted for the wind.

"You happy with that, Stone?"

"I'm good," said Harvey. "If I miss, I'll just walk over there and beat the-"

"Live firing on my command," said Melody. "You have one minute to take the shooter down, soldier." She paused as Harvey lowered his eye to the scope. "Go."

Melody waited patiently for Harvey to find his rhythm. She was pleased with his progress and looked on lovingly as, for once, he was out of his comfort zone. He fired off the first round.

"Gently," said Melody.

The second round was snatched.

"Squeeze," she said.

The third shot was perfect. Harvey remained totally motionless until he'd fired off all ten rounds. Melody waited patiently for him to finish and give her a report.

"Shots fired. Target is down," said Harvey.

"Is the weapon safe?"

"Yes."

"Lower the weapon and stand away from it. Collect your shells and place them in the bin behind you."

Melody enjoyed the formalities of shooting. But more than

anything, she maintained the same level of safety and communication at their own home range, as complacency would more than likely cause a fatality.

"How do you think you did?" asked Melody, as Harvey stood and clicked his neck both sides.

"One group of three to the head, one group of five the chest," Harvey replied.

"And the other two?"

"Wild."

"Ready to go again?" asked Melody.

"I will be, give me a-"

"No time for that, Stone. The man you took down has been replaced. You now have fifty-seconds on target two. Five by five, head and chest, on my command."

Harvey dropped to the floor, raised the weapon, and lowered his eye.

"Is the weapon safe?" asked Melody.

Harvey checked the safety.

"Mistake. You dropped your eye, and you haven't even reloaded yet."

Harvey cursed and reloaded. The end of the muzzle of the rifle moved around as he struggled with the magazine.

"You just lost your position, Stone. Look at the end of the rifle, keep it still, keep your cool, take your time. You've got this. It's precision, it's accuracy, it's a skill, and I've seen you do it before."

"Okay," said Harvey with a little frustration. "Leave me to it."

Harvey slid the fresh magazine into the rifle as gently as he could and felt it click. He didn't hit it home with his hand. He remembered Melody's words. This is a weapon for the skilled sniper. It is not an AK-47, and he was not a terrorist. He kept his body still as he brought the rifle to his shoulder. His palm opened flat, and the rifle lay on top. Melody spoke to him again.

"That's good. The weapon is part of you, no part of lying there should be uncomfortable. It sits naturally in your shoulder like it was made just for you. It rests on your palm like it's weightless. You don't look through the scope, the scope shows you what you want to see."

There was silence as Harvey controlled his breathing once more.

Then softly and calmly, Melody gave the order. "Target is at one thousand metres, Stone. It's a live shooter, and only you can bring him down. Five by five on my command.

She paused. "Begin."

When Harvey had finished, he remained still until instructed to move by Melody. He wasn't one for obeying orders, but Melody insisted on effective communication on the range, and shooting was her game, not his. He was the student.

"Shots fired. Target is down."

"Is the weapon safe?" asked Melody.

"Yes."

"Lower the weapon and stand away. Collect your shells and place them in the bin behind you."

Harvey did as instructed and waited for Melody to ask how he thought he did.

"How about that breakfast?" asked Melody.

"Yeah, sure," replied Harvey. "But aren't you going to ask how I thought I did?"

"Do I need to ask?" said Melody. "Your posture was perfect. Your grip was exactly right. You were breathing like you were reading a book instead of shooting a gun, and your timing was impeccable." She looked up at him with her hands on her hips. "If you didn't get five by five that time, I'm going to buy you a catapult. You want to go check?"

Harvey looked at the target, a small dot at the edge of the field.

"It'll still be there when we get back, won't it?" He whistled for Boon and collected the rifle from the blanket on the ground.

A few minutes later, once the rifle had been locked away, they made their way along the long muddy driveway.

Boon ran ahead, but never strayed too far, and never ran in the road. Harvey had seen his owner killed by a terrorist the year before and had rescued the dog. It was Melody who took care of him mostly, feeding him and talking to him, but the dog saw Harvey as the alpha and hung on his every word.

They walked side by side along the lane, with Boon scampering along in the fields alongside them. The morning was fresh, but the pale blue sky promised a day of pleasant sun.

Harvey was quiet, not broody, but just deep in thought. Melody eyed him. She understood him well. It had taken a long while, but she could read Harvey, although, often, that wasn't always a good thing.

He'd come a long way, she thought, from the hitman she'd met a few years before to who he was now. Melody had seen him turn, seen him struggle with his past, and fight the system only to overcome his restraints. She admired the way he hadn't given in to the system that could have locked him away for the rest of his life. Instead, he'd bent the steel framework of conformity to suit himself, and managed to come out clean. He'd left the past behind. Although gnarly hands had held him and thick chains had bound him to the criminal world, he'd broken free and come out fighting. She likened him to a magnificent sailboat that crested the high waves of the rough stormy seas and crashed into the deep troughs that threatened to swallow him. He'd weathered the storm all his life and was now enjoying the gentle breeze that pushed him along the calm, blue waters.

"Do you miss it?" asked Melody.

"Miss what? The team or the work?"

"Both, I guess," replied Melody. "It was a big part of our lives."

"Yeah, but let's face it, it couldn't have lasted much longer."

"Why not? We were doing well."

"*Doing well?*" said Harvey, incredulous. "We reported in to a bent cop, you were kidnapped and nearly drowned, I was shot at, tortured and nearly blown up, and Denver-"

"Yeah, what about him?" said Melody.

"Do I need to say it?"

"No. No, I guess you don't."

They turned out of the lane, crossed the road and stepped onto the beach. Boon was there playing in the long grass and waiting for them.

"We had the skills though," said Melody.

"Yeah, we had the skills, but not the numbers, and certainly not the direction."

"So you don't miss it?"

"No," said Harvey. "No, I don't think I do. I was ready to relax and enjoy my retirement a long time ago."

"But you're young and capable."

"And tired, Melody. Tired of the games, the lies, and most of all, I guess I'm tired of death."

There was a silence between them, as they both thought about the people they'd known that had been killed, the targets they had killed themselves, and the victims that had suffered horrible deaths.

"I'd go back," said Melody.

"You what?"

"I'd go back. Don't get me wrong, I love what we have here, but if the opportunity came knocking, I think I'd open the door."

"I thought you wanted to write?" said Harvey.

"I do, but I miss the thrill of the chase, the research, and the satisfaction of stopping..." She paused. "I don't know. It's just speculation."

"You do what you have to do, Melody. I'm staying right here."

"I gave up a lot to come be with you."

"I didn't ask you to, Melody. *You* made that choice."

"I know, I'm sorry. I shouldn't have brought it up."

"You have freedom of speech," said Harvey. He gave her a smile. "I'd support you, you know that. But I don't have the will anymore."

Melody took his hand. "Maybe you don't have the will because there isn't any danger?"

"What's that supposed to mean?"

"Oh, come on, Harvey. I saw you in action. The more peril there was, the more dangerous you got."

"I did what had to be done."

"You did some crazy stuff, Harvey."

"Whatever, we're alive, aren't we?"

"I guess. And what are the chances of opportunity knocking at the door out here?"

Harvey stopped, and Melody turned to him.

"Pretty good, I'd say," said Harvey.

"Sorry? What?"

"Blue saloon outside the café."

Melody spun and saw the car parked outside the small café.

"You're paranoid."

"I hope you're right."

"Are we going inside?" asked Melody.

"You're damn right we're going in."

CHAPTER THREE

"How did you sleep, Mrs Turvey?" said the man with the gravelly voice. He swept his side parting of fine silver hair to one side and watched as Angie Turvey struggled against her restraints. "I do hope you won't be a nuisance, Mrs Turvey," said the man. "I'd hate for you to end up like poor old Julie there."

"You sick bastard. Let us go," Angie whispered, trying not to wake her daughter, who had cried herself to sleep beside her on the large U-shaped couch.

"No can do I'm afraid. Wheels are in motion. But fear not, it'll all be over in a few days, and you'll be free to leave."

"A few days? Let her go," hissed Mrs Turvey, gesturing at her sleeping daughter. "She's done nothing wrong."

"No, but she's valuable to me," said the man. "The question is, Mrs Turvey, how valuable are you both to good old Mr Turvey?"

"What's my husband got to do with this?"

"It's too early for all this. Why don't we have coffee first? I'll make it." He grinned, then stood and walked to the kitchen like the house was his own.

Mrs Turvey sat and studied her restraints. Her wrists were

bound by layers of thick duct tape, as were her ankles. She thought about hopping to the garden, but couldn't get far even if she *could* get up from the soft couch.

The second man was younger and of Arabic descent, not local, maybe Egyptian, thought Mrs Turvey, He was sat in a chair by the dining table working on a laptop, making sure to face the screen away from her, so she couldn't see what he was looking at.

"I had a thought, Mrs Turvey," said the older man as he re-entered the room. "I know you but you don't know me." He set the tray of coffee down on the coffee table, then sat and interlocked his fingers. His arms rested on his thin legs. "My name is Caesar Crowe. My friend here is Omar. Under normal circumstances I can assure you, you'd be pleased to meet me, Mrs Turvey. But I do empathise." He paused. "These aren't ordinary circumstances, are they?"

"You mentioned my husband. What do you want? I can get it, whatever it is. Is it money? I can get anything you want from us."

Crowe laughed a loud, hearty laugh. "No, Mrs Turvey, I do not need your measly wealth." He turned to Omar at the dining table. "Omar?"

"Four hundred and fifty-eight thousand in cash, another one point two million in assets," said Omar, without looking up from the screen.

"You see, Mrs Turvey, you're only worth one point seven million." His voice turned from mock friendly to cold and harsh. "My boat is worth more than that."

"So what *do* you want?" said Mrs Turvey. "Something we own?"

"Getting warmer." The fake warmth returned to Crowe's voice.

"I can't think. I don't know. Tell me, I'll get it, you can have it, whatever it is. Just let us go."

"This is a fun game." Crowe sat forward more and leaned over the table. "Why don't you keep guessing?"

Mrs Turvey's imagination ran in circles but kept coming back to the same conclusion.

"You want me?" she asked, averting her eyes.

The silver-haired man gave a hearty laugh, and then in a flash, the humour vanished from his voice. "Let's hope it doesn't come to that, Mrs Turvey."

CHAPTER FOUR

Harvey stepped past the parked blue saloon car, told Boon to sit and stay then pushed open the door to the cafe. The little bell fixed to the top of the door frame rang lightly, loud enough to alert the waitress of a new customer, but not loud enough to disturb the customers who were already seated.

There were eleven tables each with four wooden chairs set out in true French cafe style, which was, in Harvey's mind, far too close together, and the tables themselves were too small for four people to eat at comfortably. In the right-hand corner sat an elderly couple. Harvey had seen them before. The old man from the beach sat to the left of the door, watching the world wake up. Three men in cheap suits sat at the centre table. They all looked directly at Harvey and Melody.

"Let's sit," said Melody, and gave Harvey a gentle tug on his shirt. They sat at their usual table by the window to the right of the door, Harvey with his back to the wall. The waitress beamed at them as she strode from the counter to their table. "Bonjour," she said. "Are we fine today?" she asked.

"Good morning," said Melody. "Two coffees please." Then she added, "Merci," and smiled apologetically.

"Merci. I shall be right back with your coffees." The waitress left the table and reopened the view to the three men, who continued to stare at Melody.

"Is there a problem here, boys?" asked Harvey. Melody rolled her eyes.

"Subtle, Harvey, so subtle," she murmured under her breath.

The man who was sat in the centre of the three whispered something under his breath to the men either side of him, then stood and walked the ten steps to Harvey's table. He was in his late forties, slight, with intelligent eyes that lay underneath thick, bushy eyebrows.

"Miss Mills?" he asked, looking at Melody.

Melody nodded inquisitively. "Who's asking?"

"We thought so, but couldn't be sure. Apologies for putting the frights on you outside your home earlier."

"You didn't put the frights on anyone, buddy," said Harvey.

The man looked uncomfortably at Harvey. "I'm sure," he said. "Erm, may I?" He gestured at one of the spare seats at the table.

Melody nodded her head and allowed the man to drag the chair out. He sat himself down and pulled in close to the table so he could rest his arms on top and talk discreetly. His fingers interlocked, and his gaze held Melody's in a fatherly manner. Harvey noted the monogrammed cuffs on his shirt with crossed rifles on his cuff-links.

"Miss Mills, my name is Gordon, Ian Gordon, and I believe we have a common friend, a Mr Jackson?" He raised his eyebrows with the question.

Melody drew a deep breath and sat forward.

"Go on," she said.

"Well, Miss Mills, I understand that you were previously working for-"

"We all know where Melody worked," said Harvey. "We all know her history, so cut to the chase and stop wasting our time. What's all this about?"

Gordon glanced back at Harvey. "Quite so." He fumbled for the words. "Miss Mills, Mr Jackson has requested you join him in London. There's a situation that he believes you are perfectly suited for; you have a particular skill set, were the words Mr Jackson used. My colleagues and I have been sent to find you and to kindly request that you consider this an opportunity."

"Three of you?" said Harvey. "Heavy-handed, isn't it?"

"With all due respect, Mr Stone, we were warned that there may be some resistance, and believe me, for the time being, it's best if we agree that you were not part of this conversation and that I, in fact, did not meet or even lay eyes on you."

"Is that why you drove off?" said Harvey. "You didn't want to incriminate yourselves?"

Gordon turned back to Harvey with a hint of frustration, but he held his cool. "We drove off, Mr Stone, for two reasons. Firstly, yes, association with you is not recommended, not for our sakes, but for your own. Secondly, and far more importantly, behind you in the window, your partner here, Miss Mills, had a 7.62 calibre Diemaco snipe rifle aimed at us. And given her accuracy record with the weapon, we believed it would be more appropriate, and far safer, for us to instigate initial contact in a public place, such as a cafe."

"So here we are," said Harvey.

"Quite right," replied Gordon. "May I continue please, Mr Stone?"

Harvey sat back, put his arms behind his head, and gave a slight nod. He eyed the other two men in his peripheral vision. They were feigning being relaxed. If they were who Harvey thought they were, they'd be carrying, and ready to jump into action in a fraction of a second.

"So, Miss Mills," continued Gordon, "I'm afraid I really can't say any more than that at this point. But if you'd care to join us for a briefing, I'm sure Mr Jackson will be able to fill you in on the rest of the details."

Melody held Gordon's eyes. "You want me to come with you to London based on a request from someone I used to know to do a job that I know nothing about?"

Gordon stood and replaced the chair under the table. He straightened his tie, adjusted his cuffs, and gave a cursory glance to his colleagues.

"Miss Mills, I believe we both know that you'll be there. You know the place. But I must stress, time is of the essence." Gordon glanced at his wristwatch. "We'll see you there at eight am tomorrow." He gave a tilt of his head and a confident smile. "Au revoir."

The three men left the cafe, climbed into the blue saloon, and drove off slowly.

Melody and Harvey sat in silence as the waitress brought their coffees. "Apologies for the delay, I did not want to interrupt."

"Merci," said Melody.

Harvey straightened in his seat and sat forward. "You've got twenty-two hours to get packed and into London. We both know you're going, so just go."

Melody felt the uncomfortable pause.

"You're not okay with this, are you?" replied Melody.

"It doesn't matter what I am. If it's what you want, then stopping you doing it isn't a solution that's going to work out well for either of us, is it?"

"I don't *have* to go," said Melody.

Harvey smiled and leaned forward. "What we have is great, Melody. But you're young, this could be the chance you need. Don't let *me* hold you back."

"But *you're* not holding me back. *I* am," said Melody. "I'm holding myself back because *I* want to be with you. *I* want the all the things we planned for, the things we talk about, the house, the lifestyle, and if you hadn't noticed, I want you."

Harvey ignored Melody's hidden plea for an emotional response.

"Where were those guys from?" he asked. "They seemed a little more serious than Frank ever was."

"I'm guessing MI6," replied Melody. "If they're on orders from Jackson, they must be."

"*Jackson?* MI6?"

"Must be. When the team split up, we all went in different directions. Rumour has it, Jackson was MI5, and was transferred."

"Just remember me, Melody."

"You're talking like it's *over*."

"Well, it probably *is*."

"Why is it?" Melody's face dropped. Her eyes watered. She reached over and squeezed Harvey's hand tight.

"If us ending is what it's going to take to get you to go and earn yourself an amazing career, Melody, then we're over. Go home, get your stuff, and go."

"You don't mean that," snapped Melody, louder than needed. The old couple in the corner turned at the sudden outburst, and then looked away in unison.

Harvey stood, left ten euros on the table, and walked to the door.

"I'll take the long way home. Be gone when I get back." He paused to look at her one last time. "Good luck, Melody. You earned this."

Harvey called for Boon to follow and let the cafe door close behind him. He turned left toward the village and was out of sight by the time Melody had gathered her senses and walked out into the empty street.

CHAPTER FIVE

"I knew you'd come," said a familiar voice. Melody looked up from her phone. There were no messages from Harvey. She'd checked at every opportunity since arriving in London the previous night.

"Jackson, hi," said Melody. "It's good to see you."

"I wish it could be under more accommodating circumstances," said Jackson.

Melody found her throat closed. She murmured a quiet, "me too."

"You okay?" asked Jackson.

Melody took a long breath. "I'll be fine, just memories."

"Yeah, memories, eh? Who needs them?" said Jackson in an empathetic tone, before switching to a more professional voice. "Let's go. We have a space on the fifth floor for ops."

The reception inside the Secret Intelligence Service building on London's Southbank had a corporate look with shiny marble floors, and a cleansed feel but with security unlike anything Melody had ever seen. On any other day, Melody would have been in awe of the security, and filled with wonder at the secrets the grand building held. But it was all she could do to keep Harvey from the front of her mind long enough to hold half a conversation with Jackson.

Jackson led her through security, where she was given a pass to enter the security barriers, and then had her bag screened.

They took the lift in silence. Melody was fully aware of Jackson's desire to ask after Harvey, and Jackson was fully aware of Melody's desire to ask how he came to MI6.

As if by intuition, Jackson spoke. "This could have been yours, you know?" he said. "You'd have fit right in. Someone like you could have made waves."

Melody continued to face forward.

"My wave-making days are over, Jackson. I'm happy enough." She doubted the words even before they left her lips. "Besides, you burned your way through MI5. I'm sure someone had their eyes on you long before the team split."

Jackson was saved by the doors opening. They stepped out into a quiet corridor. Melody expected a hive of activity with phones ringing and people running in every direction. Instead, the corridors were as corporate as the reception had been, shiny and clean, but bland.

The large control room with screens lining the rear wall, however, was humming with activity. Jackson closed the door behind them both. A few people looked up from their desks, others kept their heads down. It looked as if everyone was too busy to be inquisitive. Melody knew the layout. Comms were in the centre of the room, two researchers sat at one end of the room with Gordon and the two men who had accompanied him to France, and techs were sat beneath the wall-mounted screens. Melody's eyes glanced across the screens and finally rested on a familiar interface. It was LUCY, a hardware and software solution designed and built by the tech guy from her old team, Reg.

"Is that-"

"LUCY?" said Jackson. "Of course it is, LUCY doesn't go anywhere without her owner."

The chair beneath LUCY span round and Melody laid eyes on her old friend.

"Reg, oh my God. How are you?"

Reg beamed and put his blueberry muffin on his desk. He stood and the two of them hugged. Melody felt her throat close once more. It felt good to see Reg; the two had grown quite close, and then everything had changed. They hadn't seen each other for six months.

"Okay, break it up," said Jackson. "You'll have time to catch up later. In the meantime, Mills, you'll need to be briefed."

"See ya later, alligator," said Reg with a smile.

Melody smiled weakly at Reg and followed Jackson into a glass meeting room.

"Excuse the fishbowl. It won't take ten minutes to bring you up to speed, but you'll need to sign the Non-Disclosure Agreements." He slid her a pile of papers, neatly stacked with highlights beside each signature box.

"You're aware of where you are?"

"MI6?"

"It's more than that. The building is called the Secret Intelligence Service building, so it has few more tricks up its sleeve than just us. And you're aware of who the boss is?"

"No, I'm not up to date," said Melody honestly.

"Okay. Well, there are tiers and arms and all the complexities of a government organisation." Jackson gestured at the room outside. "This particular arm reports into a man called Bernard Turvey."

"Okay," said Melody, "and he's head-hunted me?"

"No, Mills, I've head-hunted you."

"So where does Turvey fit into all this?"

"He's a good man, plays the game, runs risks, wins mostly,

and he's respected, at least in this room he's well respected. Maybe not so by his peers. But that's a good thing, for him anyway."

"He's in trouble?" asked Melody.

"It's sensitive, Mills."

"Hence the secrecy act," said Melody, nodding at the pile of papers.

"He has a wife and daughter. The daughter, Anya, is eight. The wife is thirty-nine. They flew to Dubai two days ago, where the family own a holiday home on Palm Jumeirah. They haven't been seen since. No contact."

"So it's a missing person case? Bit heavy for you guys?"

"The neighbour, a family friend, is also missing, last seen heading to the Turvey's house to drop off some groceries." Jackson paused to let Melody build the scene in her head. "Have you ever heard of Caesar Crowe?"

"No, not that I remember anyway."

"Long time criminal, thinks of himself as an international mastermind, slippery, if you know what I mean?"

Melody nodded.

"We received a message from him with certain demands. Failure to complete the demands will result in the death of Turvey's family."

Jackson made the statement with an air of nonchalance that took Melody by surprise initially. But the truth *was* that it was black and white.

"What are the demands?" asked Melody. "Cash?"

"Slightly more serious than that I'm afraid." Jackson sat forward and looked Melody in the eye. "In two days' time, Bernard is due to give a speech for a charity he chairs. The speech will be televised and broadcast around the world on the usual media platforms. It's all in aid of the DWC's annual dona-tion stunt, but the allocation of funds is set to change the lives of millions of people. The donation is well received and is long awaited by all accounts."

Jackson hesitated and watched as Melody's brow furrowed, trying to figure out where she came into the situation.

"Following his speech, Bernard Turvey is to put a gun to his own head and kill himself. Live across the planet."

Melody's jaw dropped. She was stunned. "I never-"

"None of us *expected* it, Mills," said Jackson. "But the fact of the matter is if he doesn't go through with it, his family dies. Either way, they'll never see each other again."

The situation rolled around Melody's mind, but she didn't reply. There was nothing to say.

"Melody," said Jackson, the charm and friendliness lost from his tone, "we need you to take Crowe out."

Melody dizzied at the thought of what was happening. The realisation of where she was and what she was being asked to do came crashing home.

"Are you okay, Mills? You seem a little distracted," said Jackson.

"Yeah," said Melody, "I'm fine."

"Fine? What did Harvey think of you getting involved?"

"I think it's best for both of us if we leave my private life out of this," replied Melody, a little harsher than she meant. "I'm sorry, it's just-"

"It's okay. It's a sensitive case, but if you have your own issues, now would be a good time to say so. We can try and find someone else."

"I don't have issues, Jackson. Just drop it, okay. I'm in."

"Glad to hear it. You'll be in and out in no time, all being well. Now go see Ladyluck, and she'll provide the details of your alias. She's the girl on the end desk."

"An alias?" replied Melody. "Is that necessary?"

"Melody, you're a former operative for several variations of

British covert ops and armed police. The moment you step off the plane, you'll have eyes all over you. It's best if you're an unknown. I believe you'll be a Miss LeFleur. Ladyluck over there has an entire profile on you. Memorise it on the way to the airport. Oh, and Melody..."

Jackson hovered, waiting for her to respond, and for her eyes to meet his.

"It is *imperative* that the local government do *not* become aware of your presence."

CHAPTER SIX

"I want to talk to him," said Mrs Turvey. "I have to tell him-"

"Tell him you love him?" said Crowe. "How touching. But Angie, come on. Just imagine how hard it is for him right now. Can you imagine the suffering he is going through?"

Angie Turvey sobbed aloud. "I have to at least..." Her voice trailed off into a high-pitched whine.

"I'm a patient man, Angie, but please, let's keep the language to English. I don't understand whatever that is."

"You sick bastard. What's he ever done to you?" spat Angie.

"Mummy, I'm scared. What's wrong?" Anya had woken and found her hands bound just like her mother's.

"Nothing sweetheart. It's okay."

"But you're upset. What's happening? Why are we tied up?"

Angie looked up at Crowe. "Can I take her away to talk to her?"

"Ha, honestly? No, Angie, you can't."

"How am I supposed to talk to you about all this in front of her?"

"Talk about what, Mummy? What's happening?" The girl broke into a wail.

"That's just it, Angie, you're not. There's nothing to talk about."

"Is something wrong with Daddy?"

"No, baby. Nothing's wrong, please, adult talk okay? Go back to sleep. There's nothing to worry about."

"Everything is wrong, Anya," said Crowe. "You might as well know the truth."

"Don't you dare say a word to her," hissed Angie. "That's not your place. It's bad enough."

"Your father has been a very bad man, Anya."

Crowe's voice was that of an educated man with clear pronunciation, and the holier-than-thou tones of the upper class. An English, public school boy in his youth, Crowe had fallen from grace and had been lurking in the criminal underworld ever since. He used his education, wit and cunning to manipulate his newfound peers who, in his mind, all suffered from a severe lack of intelligence, which made them mere tools in his plans, as opposed to partners, colleagues or equals of any description. Caesar Crowe had no equal.

"Stop it. I swear to God I'll-"

"What did Daddy do?" asked the child.

"You'll what? Hurt me?" Crowe laughed once. It was a short, sharp laugh, empty of emotion. "Do you want to know what your daddy did, Anya?"

"No, please stop. I'll do anything, just...please," cried Angie.

"Mrs Turvey, I can assure you, you have nothing I want." He eyed her with distaste. "However, Omar here might have a different opinion."

"Please, Mr Crowe, not my daughter. Don't touch my daughter. I'll do what you want. Do what you want to me, but leave her."

"Relax, Angie. Nobody is going to touch your daughter. Do you think we're sick?"

Crowe smoothed his shirt and picked a loose thread of cotton from his trousers.

"Why don't you take her to the bedroom and let her have a lie-down, Omar?"

Omar strode across the room, and Angie caught his eye. "Don't you touch her, just, don't." Her face softened. Helplessness washed across her eyes. "Please, not her."

"I promise I will not hurt your daughter," said Omar genuinely.

"Thank you," whispered Angie.

Omar bent and picked Anya from the couch. She lay over Omar's shoulder like a sack, unable to manoeuvre into a comfortable position.

Angie felt helpless watching a stranger take her daughter away, but somehow the look Omar had given her was as reassuring as it could have been. Besides, Angie didn't want Anya to hear anything about her father from Crowe. As soon as Omar had left the room, Angie whispered to Crowe. "Please let her go. She can't see all this. It'll scar her for life."

"You want me to open the door and let her walk out?"

Angie let her head hang. She was cried out and exhausted. "Why, Mr Crowe? Why us?"

"Simple," said Crowe. "Your husband killed my family. He stole everything we had, and he ruined my life. So now..." Caesar Crowe smiled a cruel smile, and his cold grey eyes glistened. "*I'm* going to ruin *his* life."

CHAPTER SEVEN

"Your flights are booked, visa on arrival. We have an ally who will meet you at the airport. From there, he'll take you to get equipped, though I believe Tenant also has a few tricks up his sleeve that you'll take in your hand luggage. Nothing out of the ordinary."

Melody shot a glance through the glass partition to Reg, who sat drinking coke at his desk, leaning back with his keyboard on his lap and his feet up on a stool. Reg must have sensed Melody's look, as he turned in his seat, smiled and waved.

"Who's the ally?" asked Melody.

"Bob," said Jackson.

"*Bob?*" replied Melody. "Is that his full name or is there more to it than that? Maybe another syllable or something?"

"That's all you'll need to know. He's taking a pretty big risk getting you armed out there, so the less you know about him, the better. He'll find you at the airport."

"So he's not operational?" asked Melody. "He's not helping us?"

"He's engaged elsewhere. We have a small team out there.

The entire population of the country is only nine million, so the team tends to reflect that." Jackson held her gaze. "You'll be on your own, Mills."

"No local help? Police? The UAE has pretty effective security council from what I hear."

"Mills, it's important that we stop this man. I'm sure you empathise with the sensitivities?"

"Of course. It's a shocking demand."

"What's also important, politically, is that the Dubai government don't find out that we're there."

Melody didn't reply. She stared at Jackson, interpreting what was not said, rather than what was.

"That's why you chose me, isn't it?" said Melody. "Because if I'm caught with a weapon, or for whatever else, there's no tie."

"Mills, it's not-"

"Am I using my own passport? Or will I be masquerading as some fictitious do-gooder out on a lonely holiday in the desert?"

"Have you finished?" said Jackson.

"No, I'm just getting started."

"Well, I'll finish it for you," said Jackson, taking control of the briefing. "There's a long-standing treaty between the UAE and the UK governments. We're allies, but recently that tether has been under some pressure. Officially, we're supposed to request permission to send in an operative. But that takes time, which as you're well aware, we do not have."

"And if they do find out we're there?"

Jackson stared hard at her. "We're not there, Mills. We don't even know you. If the Dubai government gets wind of what we're doing, it won't be us trying to patch things up, it'll be the PM and the foreign minister. And if it comes to that, well, I'm sure you can use your imagination."

There was a silence that was broken by the door to the control centre being opened. The hum in the room dropped and people lowered their heads. A man stood in the doorway wearing a sharp suit and brogues. On any other day, he would be the image of success and confidence. But on that day, his posture was weak, his eyes sunken, and his crop of jet black hair looked as though it had been hastily made good, rather than groomed and styled.

Jackson caught the man's attention, and he made his way to the door of the fishbowl meeting room where Melody and Jackson sat. Closing the door behind him, he turned to look down at Melody.

"Sir," said Jackson, "this is Mills, the operative we spoke about." Jackson turned to Melody. "Mills, this is-"

"Bernard," the man cut in. "Bernard Turvey. I'd prefer if we kept this informal. You're not an MI6 asset, rank is of no importance here. What is important is that my family are made safe."

Melody shook Bernard's hand, and he sat beside Jackson. "I presume Jackson has briefed you?"

"Yes, sir. We were just getting to the details of the operation."

"Good," said Bernard. "I'll stay. There's not much to it for an operative of your calibre. Are you aware of the Palm Jumeirah in Dubai?"

"Sir, are you up to this?" asked Jackson. "We can handle it."

"The last time I looked, Jackson, I ran the operations."

Jackson nodded slowly. "As you wish, sir."

"I am aware of the Palm Jumeirah, sir, yes," said Melody.

Jackson pulled an aerial photo from the stack of papers in the centre of the desk and pointed to the frond H, which was on the south side of the man-made island.

"You can see here that each frond represents a branch of the Palm. Residential villas line both sides of each frond, giving each villa its own beach access. The beaches are private and accessible only from the villas themselves, or by sea. Frond H is situated here." Jackson used his pen as a pointer. "And the Turvey villa is located here." Jackson circled the villa before moving to frond G. "We have secured the rental of a holiday home on frond G, which is here." Jackson pointed again at the adjacent frond and circled another villa. "As you can see, it's not directly opposite the Turvey villa, but it's very close. It's a three-hundred metre swim across the water at high tide. Villa to villa, you're looking at an eight-hundred-metre shot."

"You want me to take him out?"

"No, Mills. We *need* you to take him out," said Jackson. "As soon as you arrive, you need to formulate a plan then get the surveillance running. Tenant will gear you up. After that, you'll have just under twenty-four hours to take him out."

"Is he alone?"

"We don't know. We assume accomplices, but these will be financially motivated if there are any. Take out Crowe, and they'll lose interest."

"What if I take out Crowe and the accomplices do something stupid?"

"Mills," said Bernard, "don't *let* them do anything stupid."

"Bob will arrange a Diemaco for you," said Jackson, "your weapon of choice, and he'll set you up in the villa. From there, you're on your own. See Tenant before you leave for your comms and surveillance gear. See Ladyluck, and she'll set you up with your ID and travel documents, all expenses paid, but be sensible. You know the rules. Any questions?"

"Yes," said Melody.

Jackson raised his eyebrows, waiting for her to speak.

"Hypothetically, if I fail?"

Bernard swallowed and took a breath. Melody saw his tired eyes redden and shine as he fought to hold his emotions back. "If you fail, Mills, I'll be on stage in two days' time holding a Sig to my head, and saying goodbye to my family."

CHAPTER EIGHT

It had been less than twenty-four hours since Melody had left. Harvey was out running and had stopped on the beach. Boon stood far ahead looking back at him, wondering what his master was doing. He trotted back to Harvey, who then dropped to his haunches to stroke Boon's head.

Melody had left a note for Harvey on his bedside table, and for the first time in Harvey's life, he just couldn't shake the thought of a girl from his mind. He'd always been the one to end the few relationships he'd had. But this time it was different. With previous girls, he'd ended things because they were so far removed from the life he'd led, the life of a killer. It didn't matter how much he'd liked them, there just wasn't a way to explain to them what he did. He couldn't even tell them it was just transactional, it had been business; it was his job. They would never have understood, and would always wonder where he went late at night, which led to questions, which led to lies, deceit, and ultimately the end of the relationship. But he'd met Melody *because* of what he'd done for a living, and she'd fallen in love with him despite his past. He thought on that point. Fallen in love.

The note had been succinct and direct. Melody told him that she didn't believe they were over. It had all been too good to throw away. She'll be back when the job was done if Harvey would have her.

"What do we do, boy?" he asked Boon.

The dog just buried his head into Harvey, as if questioning why he'd stopped stroking him.

Harvey wanted her back, but also knew that he couldn't be the one who stopped her from reaching her potential. Melody was a great operative. He'd had every faith in her when they'd worked a job together. But questions ran through Harvey's mind. What if in ten years' time she regrets staying with him? What if someone comes after Harvey? An old enemy or a released prisoner. What if?

They had enjoyed a great six months together since they'd left the very unofficial team that had targeted organised crime in London. One of their colleagues had been killed by terrorists. Then an internal investigation had uncovered Frank Carver, their boss, as being dirty. The time to leave had been right for Harvey, but Melody had higher aspirations. She had worked her way up through the ranks and shone. Harvey stared at the sand. He couldn't be the one to hold her back.

When he stepped back into the house and closed the door behind him, the place felt emptier than ever before. Dishes sat on the draining board in the kitchen, pictures hung on the wall, and cushions were placed neatly on the little two-seater couch opposite the wood-burning stove. They were all reminders of Melody. Harvey would never hang pictures, and he'd never buy cushions from little boutique stores. He'd always lived a simple life. Possessions had never been high on his agenda. But now he'd had them, now he'd had Melody, he found he wanted them. He wanted her.

What if she was hurt? What if she was killed because she

was sent to do a job that he could have stopped? If she didn't do it, someone else would. Let them, Harvey thought. Let Melody stay safe.

There were no messages on his phone from Melody, and he hadn't sent any to her, despite the part of his mind that fed memories of her into his thoughts. He'd wanted the change to be as easy as possible for her. Harvey stood in limbo between the bedroom and the living room. Boon stared up at him, sensing his master's unease.

Then, without any further hesitation, the decision was made. Sitting on the edge of the bed, with Boon at his heels, he lifted his phone and dialled a number he'd memorised.

Jackie and George were retired British expats enjoying the autumn years of their life on France's southern coast. Melody and Harvey had met them in the village and Melody had said they seemed kind, genuine and trustworthy, and the foursome had informally arranged to go to dinner, with no date set. Harvey made the call. They agreed to look after Boon for a few days, and when he got back from his trip, they'd all go to dinner. Harvey hoped it would as a foursome.

Less than two hours later, Harvey was on his motorbike blasting through the lanes, and then onto the motorway that would take him to Calais. He'd made the journey many times before. In the past, he'd stop at an Air B&B or bed-and-breakfast to make the journey last two days, both for comfort and to enjoy the road. But this time, he rode directly to London, only stopping for fuel, toilet and water breaks.

He made the journey in fifteen hours, and climbed off the bike sore and stiff.

The winter days in London are short, and night falls quickly. Workers arrive to work in the dark and leave in the dark. This worked in Harvey's favour. He'd waited an hour for his target to show, and the dark would allow him to get close without being seen.

The man walked down the steps of his office onto the Albert Embankment and turned to head towards the train station. Harvey followed on foot. Vauxhall Station was a five-minute walk, and as Harvey shadowed the man, he made a plan. It wasn't until the man stepped onto the packed train and reached up for the handle to steady himself that Harvey stepped up behind him. The doors closed with a hiss. People fought for space to read their newspapers and books. Others stared at their phones. Harvey moved in closer to Reg and spoke quietly in his ear.

"Don't turn around," said Harvey. "Where is she?"

Reg startled and began to turn.

"I said, don't turn around," said Harvey. "Where is she?"

"You missed her," said Reg. "She's on her way."

"Where, Reg?"

"I can't say. I signed the-"

"Reg."

"Dubai. But you didn't hear it from me."

"You have her location; tell me where to find her."

"Harvey, you can't, the assignment, it's serious."

"Even more reason for me to go bring her out of there, don't you think?"

The train braked hard as it reached the next station, and when the doors opened, Harvey found himself blocking the exit. He stubbornly stayed where he was, forcing other passengers to move around him.

"Are you going to move or what, mate?" said a construction worker in dirty jeans, heavy boots, and a thick jacket.

Harvey didn't reply.

The man put his head down as soon as he made eye contact with Harvey and edged around him.

"Still got your charm, Harvey," said Reg, as more people replaced the ones that disembarked.

Harvey and Reg moved to the far side of the train to stand out of the way of the hurried commuters.

"It's good to see you, Harvey."

Reg's words were met with Harvey's stony face. "I need to find her."

"Her flight left a few hours ago, Harvey," said Reg. "I'm sorry. I can't bring her back."

"How long has she gone for?"

"It's a two-day op," said Reg. "I can call you as soon as she's back if you want?"

"You can do better than that, Reg," said Harvey. "Set me up with comms and give me access to her tracker, and I'll go find her myself."

"Seriously, Harvey, it's out of the question."

"Have you forgotten exactly what it is I did for a living, Reg?"

Reg shook his head. "How could I forget that?"

"Right, comms and tracker. Where and when?"

"I'm not going to win this, am I?" said Reg.

Harvey didn't reply.

"Tomorrow night. Same place same time?" said Reg.

"That's too late. I'll be twenty-four hours behind."

"I can't get the comms until tomorrow morning."

"What about her tracker?"

"You could just download the app."

"The app?"

"Don't worry, it's encrypted," said Reg. "It'll give you access to LUCY. From there, you'll see where Melody is."

"What's your stop?"

"It's the next one."

"Okay, we're going outside, set me up with the app."

"You're really going out there?" asked Reg. "You could compromise the whole operation."

"Reg, when have you ever known me to do anything stupid?"

"Well, there was the time you jumped out of the moving van onto the moving taxi and got yourself run over. And, of course, there was the time you jumped into the Thames wearing an explosive vest. And-"

"Reg, stop," said Harvey. "I'm not going out to get involved, I'm going out there to watch Melody and make sure she stays safe."

Reg nodded slowly. "The company man inside me hates this. I want to call this in."

"But?"

"But the friend inside me wants to go look after her. This one is serious."

The train braked again, and the doors hissed open. "Shall we?" said Reg. "Let's go ruin my career."

They walked to the top of the steps and surfaced at Clapham Common.

"Okay, give me your phone, I'll set it up," said Reg.

"Not here," replied Harvey. "Have you forgotten who you work for? There's a bench on the common near the church. Take my phone, walk clockwise around the grass, and I'll meet you on that bench." Harvey handed Reg his phone.

Reg looked at Harvey's phone. "Wow, you really need to update this beast, Harvey. I'm surprised it even-" Reg turned around to face Harvey, but he was gone.

CHAPTER NINE

By the time Harvey was stepping onto the plane and taking his seat at the very back, Melody had already landed and was walking confidently through terminal three of Dubai International Airport. She scanned the crowds that were waiting for loved ones or colleagues to arrive but saw nobody she recognised and nobody that wore the serious look of an operative. She didn't imagine the mysterious Bob would be standing and holding a card with her name on, but she thought she might have been able to spot an operative.

She exited the terminal and looked around. It was winter, but the air was still warm compared to the frigid bite of London's perpetual breeze. Decorative fountains welcomed newcomers to the country, along with rows of taxis and limousines.

"Excuse me, do you have the time?" said a voice.

Melody turned to see a short, stocky western man stride towards her. She glanced at her watch. "It's two am," she replied with a smile.

"Okay, thanks," said the man. "Get in a cab, and then check

your pocket," he added under his breath and disappeared into the throng of people. Melody did just that.

"Just drive," she said to the taxi driver. "I'll tell you where shortly." She turned on the interior light and pulled a piece of yellow notepaper from her pocket. The scribbled writing was just an address. She expected nothing more.

"Al Warqa," Melody said to the driver. "Street sixteen."

The cab driver nodded and fought his way across three lanes of traffic onto a faster road, then accelerated to one hundred and twenty kilometres an hour. His driving was erratic and not at all relaxing, as if the driver was keen to drop her off so he could get another fare; passenger comfort was not high on his list of priorities.

In the early hours of the morning, the roads were clear. A glance at the compass app on her phone told Melody she was heading east. She knew that the Palm Jumeirah was south and west of the airport. She kept an eye on the compass and the GPS, and soon, as the buildings grew smaller and fewer, the dark landscape outside was represented by yellow desert on her phone's map.

Villas lined the street, each of them hidden away behind tall walls. She directed the driver to stop three hundred yards from the villa on the address and waited for him to pull away before walking to the front gate. The empty street felt open and insecure; she felt an element of vulnerability. The gate was open, so she stepped inside onto the forecourt and pushed the little gate closed behind her. The villa was a single storey with a large, wooden double door, which was ornately decorated. It opened as she climbed the few marble steps, and Melody stepped inside.

Melody was immediately hit by the coolness of the house. High ceilings and sparse windows kept the Arabic houses cool, and the constant air conditioning maintained the temperature.

The marble continued throughout the interior, along a wide hallway which led into an open space where the man who had asked her the time at the airport stood waiting.

"Miss LeFleur?"

"You'd be in trouble if I wasn't," replied Melody.

"Welcome to Dubai. I'm Bob," said the man. "Apologies about the airport, can't be too careful, you know?"

"It's okay, I enjoyed the ride."

"Drink?" asked Bob. "Wine, whiskey or water?"

"Is the water safe to drink?"

"Safer than the wine." Bob smiled. "It's all bottled."

"I'll take a water then, thanks."

"Relax," said Bob. "You want to take a shower before we get down to business?"

"When are we leaving?"

"For the Palm? In a couple of hours, you'll need to beat the traffic," said Bob as he stepped into the kitchen.

Melody looked around at the Peli-cases stacked up against the walls. Bob came back into the room and followed her gaze.

"Not for you," he said. "Your kit is in the next room." He passed Melody the chilled water.

Melody nodded. "Thanks."

"Take a shower," said Bob. "The spare bedroom is through that door. There're towels and stuff. When you're done, I'll brief you and get you kitted up."

Thirty minutes later, Melody was sitting crossed legged on the floor of the majlis, an area with floor cushions around the edge where locals socialise. Two large, intricately designed rugs covered the majlis floor. Bob handed her two large Peli-cases; one was long and slender and one was the size of a small suitcase.

"Seven-point-six-two Diemaco with rounds and scope in one case, and SIG Sauer, comms, binos, and bugs in the other," said Bob, as he lowered himself to the floor with a bottle of beer.

Melody popped each case open and checked the kit. She trusted Bob, but if she didn't check and a mistake happened, she wouldn't be in a position to point fingers.

"Do you have a map for me?" she asked.

Bob reached across and handed her a thin folder. "All the info we can give you."

"Do we have eyes on the house at all?"

"None. The location isn't even confirmed, but it's the best we have."

"The location isn't confirmed?" said Melody.

"Apparently the demands were sent over an encrypted line via a dozen different locations worldwide. HQ didn't even have a position until some tech guy decrypted the message and traced it back around the world."

Melody thought of Reg and had faith in his ability. "I'm pretty sure it's fine then. Did you see the villa I'm going to hole up in?"

"Yeah, I rented it. I had a good look around. No nosy neighbours, it's mainly holiday rentals on the Palm. There are some permanent residents but not many. The Turveys' house is supposed to be on the other side of the water, and about four or five houses along. You'll need to do a recce yourself."

Melody put the file down. "Doesn't seem like there's much concrete here."

"There's not," said Bob. "But what can we do?"

"Are you joining in the fun?"

Bob shook his head. "No chance. I can't blow my cover. You'll be on your own, I'm afraid."

Melody nodded. "What's the situation like here?"

"Situation?"

"In Dubai? Do you see much action?"

"No, we're forbidden to operate here. I'm just keeping the place warm," replied Bob, easing himself back. He was clearly comfortable with his posting.

"You must be bored then. Don't you want to get involved?"

"Not really, we've got too much to lose. I'm guessing Jackson explained the tension?"

"Yeah, he said we couldn't get caught," said Melody.

"No, he said I can't get caught," said Bob. "You can do as you wish. You're not tied to anything."

"How am I getting there?"

"I'll take you. That'll be the last you see of me. After that, you're on your own." Bob finished his beer and reached for another from a six-pack beside him.

"Are you on your own out here?" asked Melody.

"Listen, LeFleur, or whatever your name is," Bob said, sitting forward to hold her gaze, "you seem nice, you're pretty, and I hear good things about you. But don't go cocking this up. Stop asking questions and get your head in the game. *You don't need to know* how many there are of us out here *or* what our real names are, and when I drop you off, you'd do well to forget you ever met me. I'll be civil and professional. I suggest you do the same. There's more than just your own life at stake here."

Melody absorbed the hit with raised eyebrows and slammed the peli-cases shut. "So now I know where I stand, why don't we hit the road?" said Melody. "I've exhausted this resource, time to move on and get the game in play."

"Don't take it personally, LeFleur, and trust me, the game is already in play. You're coming up to bat in the last quarter. All eyes are on you, girl."

CHAPTER TEN

"Sir, I just had a check in from Mills. She's in the villa and setting up," said Reg.

"Good, let's get eyes on her if we can," said Jackson. "I want to see what we're up against."

Reg began typing effortlessly fast into his keyboard. He was using the chat feature he'd added to LUCY, his creation.

"Sir, she's just prepping for a recce. She's setting up the camera with night vision, so we'll see her swim across."

"Right, everybody, listen in," said Jackson, addressing the whole room. "Up until now, we've been going on hearsay and chasing our tail. We now have an asset in place, and pretty soon, we'll have audio on the Turvey house. We need voice recognition ready to go. Get the databases up. We need eyes and ears on the local police. I want to know the moment they get wind of something. We cannot be found operating in Dubai, people. Lastly, I need everyone switched on. If you need coffee, go get it now. If you need the washroom, do what you've got to do because once that audio is on, and the clock starts counting down, you won't have five minutes to spare." Jackson paused.

"We've got this. We can stop him, but timing will be critical. So keep alert."

There was a hustle as people prepared for the long shift. Some had already been there for more than a full day; others had taken the time to get some rest. Jackson approached Reg who sat with his feet up and his keyboard on his lap.

"What are you up to, Tenant?"

"I'm lining up access to the Dubai roads authority, the RTA. From there, I'll be able to follow someone by road, for example, Melody, as she runs to the airport."

"Ok, good. Is that live?" asked Jackson.

"No, I'm just setting up the access. Once we're in, there's a good chance of being caught and the web traffic being traced back here. So we won't use it until we need it."

"Good. How long will it take to initialise a connection?"

"Depends. All I can do for now is prep it ready to go. Likewise for the security council. I can get all sorts in there, but until we need it, I don't see the need to make a grand entrance and announce our arrival."

"Good stuff," said Jackson. "How's Mills doing?"

Reg flicked his mouse across two of his screens and revealed a high-quality camera view of a small stretch of water with large houses lining the far side. "That's the Turvey's house there," said Reg, "the one with the kayaks on the beach and the swing set."

"Is that the best we can do?" asked Jackson. "We're not going to be able to see much of Mills."

"Hopefully nor is our man, Crowe, sir," replied Reg.

"If she's as good a shot as you say, this will be over in the next few hours. As soon as the sun comes up, I want that audio recording, and I want Mills in place ready to pull the trigger."

Jackson left Reg to it and headed to the small glass meeting room. He closed the door behind him and pulled up the recently dialled numbers on his phone. The ringtone was halted by a strong, elderly man's voice. "Jackson, fill me in," came the reply.

Jackson pictured the old man sitting on the floor above with a tumbler of brandy, his old squashed and pitted nose, huge eyebrows, and a smugness that came from a life of entitlement.

"Sir, all assets are in play," said Jackson. "Mills is in place. We're setting up audio tonight. Our man Omar will venture outside on our signal and take Melody by surprise."

"Good. What about Stone?"

"He's en-route, sir."

"For sure?" said the old man. "We can't have any mistakes here."

"For sure, sir. Gordon tailed him and Tenant to Clapham Common last night. Tenant set him up with Mills' tracker. Stone left shortly after."

"Good. Remember how we need this to play out," said the old man. "I need Crowe taken out and Stone either implicated or dead. God knows we might just get out of this with our hands clean, and leave Dubai to take care of Stone."

Jackson felt a pang of uneasiness grip his stomach. He understood that Stone was a liability, and he understood that the old man held a grudge against Stone and wanted him finished. He also understood that the old man held the keys to Jackson's own career. Life wasn't always fair. There had to be winners and there had to be losers. Jackson didn't plan on being a loser.

"Leave it to me, sir," said Jackson, and he disconnected the call.

CHAPTER ELEVEN

"Can we at least have some light in here?" asked Angie Turvey. "I don't even know what time of day it is."

"You don't need to know the time of day," replied Crowe. "Why don't you tell me about your husband?"

"Where's my daughter?"

"She's safe. She's with Omar. He's great with kids; he has two of his own."

"Two of his own? How can anybody have their own kids and put someone through this ordeal?"

"Easy," said Crowe. "Money. Now tell me about your husband."

"My husband? What do you want to know? It sounds like you know enough already."

"Au contraire, Angie. Tell me about *him*." There was a finality to the last word. It sounded almost spiteful with Crowe's over-pronounced diction.

"He's my husband. He's a good man."

"He's a good man, is he?"

"Yes, yes he is. He chairs a charity in London. He helps thousands of people."

"How does he help them, Angie?" Crowe's voice had turned soft with an inquisitive tone.

"He re-homes people that need twenty-four-hour specialist care. He provides medical aid. He, he-"

"It sounds a lot like Mr Turvey knows how to spend other people's money, and make himself glow with the sheen of an angel while doing so, Angie. Tell me, does Mr Turvey ever get hands on and help these people? Does he wipe the drool from their chins? Does he hold their hands when they shiver and shake? Does he clean their soiled clothes when the treatment has its way?"

"How can he? He just organises-"

"What does he organise, Angie?"

"Help. He organises help for the people."

"Does he do the organising? I must say I find it hard to picture Mr Turvey in his fine suit, waiting on hold for a hospital clerk to respond to his call. It sounds like the type of task someone else might do for him, doesn't it, Angie? Someone like, say an assistant, or secretary. Does he have one of those? An assistant?"

"Yes, of course he does. He's far too busy to-"

"Far too busy to what, Angie? Come to little Anya's school play? Or her dance class, perhaps? What do you say, Angie? Is he too busy to take care of his wife?"

"You bastard," spat Angie. "You don't know anything about us." She struggled against the duct tape that had been wrapped around her ankles and wrists, then, like the time before that, and the time before that, she stopped fighting, and her body crumpled in defeat.

"Oh, Angie, what a performance," said Crowe. "Julie there was the same, of course, but *she* had something to fight for. *She* had a loving husband."

"*Bernard* is a loving husband."

"Ah yes, Angie. But who is it he is loving? Ah, *that's* the question, isn't it?"

"You're going to pay for this."

"Yes, probably, but you know what? I'll have a damn fun time while they try to catch me."

"You know who he is, so you know who he works for?"

"Yes, I do, and I happen to know that the United Kingdom's secret services are not permitted to operate here in the UAE without specific instructions and permission. The Sheik would not be at all happy if our boys in blue were found to be carrying out an investigation on UAE soil, let alone sending a bunch of armed SAS abseiling off the rooftops. Besides, Angie, Omar re-routed the message around the planet before it was delivered. They'll still be looking for where the message came from by the time old Bernie gets up on stage for his last performance."

"He'll find a way. He knows pe*ople."

"Yes, he does," said Crowe. "I must say, you're especially kind to him, given all he's put you through. Do you ever think about him with the other girls, Angie?"

"Shut up. Stop saying that. There *are* no other girls."

"Oh, that's strange," said Crowe. He turned to face the hallway. "Omar," he called softly, like he was summoning his puppy.

Omar crept down the stairs and stepped into the room a short while later.

"How's little Anya doing?" asked Crowe. His feigned concern sickened Angie.

"She's fine. She's sleeping," replied Omar.

"Oh good," said Crowe. "She's had a hard day, hasn't she? Poor little mite."

Nobody replied.

"Omar, would you happen to have the photos of Mr Turvey and those Russian girls to hand? You know the ones."

"Yes, they are here where you left them." Omar walked to the dining table and picked up a blue cardboard file. He handed them to Crowe.

"Now, what do we have here?" said Crowe, as he flicked through the A4 printed photos. "Ah yes, here we are. Here's Mr Turvey enjoying drinks and dinner with another of the charity board members, I believe. Do you know this man, Mrs Turvey?" He pointed to the man opposite her husband.

"Yes, he's a friend," replied Angie. "That's Eddie McIntyre."

"And who is this by his side?" asked Crowe.

"I don't know," said Angie, looking down at the floor.

"Pretty, isn't she? I bet she cost a few quid. What do you say, Omar? Pretty? Expensive?"

"Both," replied Omar from the dining table. He was working on the laptop, but Angie still couldn't see what he was doing exactly. She considered waiting for her chance and getting to the laptop herself. A mini-plan formed in her head that she'd post a help message on social media.

"And here they are going into the Dorchester Hotel, Angie," continued Crowe. "Wasn't that where he took you, Angie, all those years ago?" He tutted. "That's just plain rude."

"He has problems," said Angie. "I know what he does." Her head hung low, and her foot began to shake involuntarily. "I need to sleep and I need to pee."

"Oh, but we're just getting to the good stuff, Mrs Turvey," said Crowe with sickening enthusiasm. He held up a photo. "This one's my favourite. I thought I'd save it for last."

CHAPTER TWELVE

For Harvey, being crammed in a seat for nearly eight hours on a passenger jet was horrific. He didn't touch the in-flight entertainment and used the time to plan instead. Many scenarios emerged in his mind's eye, but one scene continued to force its way to the front among countless others, the plan of what he'd say to Melody. But each time he came close to preparing a speech, he could only imagine her being hurt by someone else. Then his mind wandered to handing out cruel punishment to whoever was harming Melody. He couldn't help but feel it was all wrong, that she shouldn't be there.

So in the end, his plan always came back to patience, planning and executing. It was the mantra of his mentor, Julios. There would be no speech, there would be no apologies, there would be no hurt. Melody would not even know Harvey was there unless she needed help. Then he'd be there, ready to step in. Until that moment, he decided he'd be a shadow, a skill he'd been honing since his early teens.

Harvey stepped off the plane onto the gangway. He didn't have a carry-on, nor did he have any checked luggage, just the clothes on his back. Passport control was interesting, so many different nationalities, all waiting to visit Dubai. Harvey wondered if he was the only one there who didn't want to see the sights.

When he reached the exit to the terminal, hundreds of people stood waiting for loved ones to arrive. Harvey strode through the crowds, aware that only Reg knew he was even in the country. Ideally, Harvey would have rented a motorbike, but the journey and the chaotic terminal had gotten the better of him, and he settled for a taxi. The cab ride gave Harvey time to study the LUCY app on his phone that Reg had installed. He hit the drop down, selected 'track' and was presented with only one available operative to track. But it was the only tracker he needed, Melody's.

She was a thirty-minute drive from the airport on Palm Jumeirah, on one of the branches of the tree-shaped island. Harvey knew the Palm Jumeirah to be an area where wealthy people lived and holidayed. He presumed there to be tight security in place.

As the cab drove him along the Palm, Harvey saw the entrances to fronds A and B, then C and D. They all had tight security. The guards themselves, lit dimly by the small light from their little cabins, didn't look particularly terrifying. But it would just take one of them to raise the alarm and the game would be up. He couldn't chance it. He'd need to circumvent the security.

In the end, the taxi dropped Harvey a few hundred yards from the entrance to frond G, where the tracker icon on the LUCY app showed Melody to be. He zoomed in on the icon, which was accurate within three metres. She was on the beach out the back of the house.

Harvey found a spot between fronds G and H where he could easily scale a wall, make his way through the landscaped vegetation, and drop down onto the beach. He stayed amongst the shrubbery for a while and practised his old habit of waiting a standard full minute before making his move. He sat at the point where fronds G and H met, with each of the private beaches in front of him, one bearing left, the other bearing right.

There was no sign of any activity. The app showed Melody to be another six hundred yards along the beach to his left. He wondered why she would be housed there. It didn't make sense. The place had so much security that fast getaways and staying invisible would be almost impossible. She must have a target, Harvey thought, and he'd have money that the target would be one of the houses on the opposite beach. But which one? The villas were all very well maintained, not Harvey's style, but he could see the appeal.

He dropped down onto the beach of frond H. The app told Harvey that Melody was still on the beach of frond G, just across the water. But she wouldn't see him in the dark on the opposite beach. He walked close to the shore so the incoming tide would remove his prints. Most of the houses looked empty, except a few. An Asian family sat at a dining table in one house, another just had a solitary man in shorts watching a movie, oblivious to Harvey outside. More houses had lights on. One had all the curtains closed, others had lights on but no sign of activity. Nothing seemed out of the ordinary. The tide had already begun to wash away his boot prints by the time he walked back along the beach, trying to piece it all together.

Harvey reached the place where the two beaches met, climbed over the rocks that separated them, and began to walk along frond G as if he was a holidaymaker out for an evening stroll. Halfway along, he glanced at LUCY and found Melody's icon to be halfway across the water. Keeping to the shadows at the back of the beach, he sat and watched for movement on the water.

He knew Melody was a strong swimmer. She could probably manage a fair amount of the three-hundred metre swim underwater. Harvey heard no splashing, saw no dark shape in the water, but knew she was out there somewhere.

On the beach outside the house, Harvey stood where LUCY had originally pinned Melody's location. The house next door had a row of thick trees and bushes, an ideal spot for him to wait and observe. It wasn't long before wet footsteps on the sand announced Melody's return. She trudged up the steps in a black wetsuit and neoprene booties then pulled the suit off and hung it to dry over the small table and chairs beside the pool. Harvey looked on from the shadows of the bushes. He was desperate to call her name or go to meet her. But he couldn't. He'd just be the distraction that caused the mistake. He was better off being an observer, a guardian. If she needed help, he'd be there. If she didn't, then he'd stay out of the way, and find the right time to tell her what he wanted to tell her.

Harvey saw the bedroom light come on at the rear of the house and knew she would be taking a shower to wash the salt off her skin. He needed more facts. He needed to know when she was going across again, so he could cross in advance and be waiting, ready. There was a small balcony at the rear of the house, adjoined to the bedroom where he presumed Melody was showering. He took the opportunity to climb up onto the ground-floor window ledge and leap up to grab the balcony, pulling himself up with ease. Once he'd confirmed that Melody was nowhere in sight, he climbed the balustrade and tucked himself into a dark corner. He chanced a glance back into the room and could see the Peli-case with the Diemaco. Another smaller case was open with a SIG, binos, night vision and a few other accessories laid across the bed.

He played out her operation in his head. She must have swum across to plant some audio or video feeds then she came back here to get set up for a long-range shot. The bathroom light went off. Harvey tucked his legs up close to his chest to stay small. The bedroom light went out.

Then the balcony door opened.

Harvey listened for movement. He smelled the familiar scent of Melody's shampoo escaping from the balcony door, luring him like a child is lured with a trail of sweets.

The sound of a table being dragged across the tiled floor told Harvey that Melody was still in the room. He closed his eyes and pictured her. If her task was to take a shot at a house on the far side of the water, she would be pulling a table up in front of the balcony to lay on and take the shot. She would have her comms on the table with her, and her binos to mark the distance. Once she was set up for the shot, Melody wouldn't move until the target presented itself.

Harvey stared out across the water to the house that she had been to. It was the house he had seen on his walk with the lights on and curtains closed. He knew her style. She would have planted audio against the glass of the house's sliding doors. The sound would carry well through the glass. He sat in the darkness, and watched the house with her, like a voyeur.

He heard Melody get comfortable on the table. He heard her prepare herself for the long haul. A shot like the one she was going to take would require concentration and focus. It felt good to be so close to her. A small part of him wished he could just reach out to her, or even say something. Then she spoke.

"I thought you wouldn't be able to stay away," said Melody. "Too tempting for you?"

Harvey's head turned, his mouth opened, but she spoke again.

"Phase one complete, Reg. Audio is on," said Melody.

Harvey didn't reply.

"I'm in position but the curtains are closed," she began. "Audio is loud and clear, but right now it's just getting snores and the hum of the air conditioning. Sounds like someone's sleeping downstairs. With any luck they'll wake up and open the curtains. Until then, I'm blind and without a shot."

The tinny voice replied something inaudible to Melody.

"I am sitting tight. I'm dug in and ready. How long do we have until the speech?"

There was a pause while her handler spoke, then, "Sixteen hours? You better hope those curtains open before then, or else we'll need a plan B."

Another pause.

"Copy. Will report back hourly. Out."

Harvey sat and listened to the one-sided conversation. Sixteen hours until a speech? He couldn't put the pieces together. The only thing Harvey could possibly do to expedite the issue would be to go and do something to make whoever it was open the curtains. He'd need Melody to leave first; he couldn't get off the balcony without her knowing he was there.

Harvey sat and waited. Sixteen hours. He'd done worse, he thought to himself, and in far worse conditions than by the beach in Dubai.

CHAPTER THIRTEEN

Jackson closed the door to his modest office. The walls were painted white, which was standard throughout the building. He'd personalised it with a few photos of him with his unit in Afghanistan, stood alongside a Challenger tank in full combats, and armed to the teeth. Another photo on his desk was of his family and their pet retriever laying together on the ground in the garden of their Sussex home.

He pulled his personal phone from his pocket and dialled a number from the recent call list. It was answered almost immediately.

"Jackson, update me," said the old man's voice with no pleasantries or salutations.

"Mills is in position, audio is set up, and we have ears. Not much to report until they wake up and open the curtains."

"And Stone?"

"Tenant put a tracker on his phone. He's hiding a few metres away from Mills."

"You brought Tenant into this? I thought I told you to keep this on the down low?"

"Tenant is helping his friend. He doesn't know we're onto him. He's not stupid. He'd know we were after Stone all along."

"So, what's your plan?"

"We stick with plan A until we have no option. It's the cleanest takedown."

"So Mills takes the shot and high tails it out of there, and we send in our asset to pick up Stone?"

"Yes. As long as somebody opens the curtains and Mills can take the shot, the play will roll, and we'll be clean."

"And plan B?" asked the old man in a long, tired mumble.

"Three hours before the speech, we send Mills over and she gets caught. Stone steps in and takes out Crowe."

"Sounds like there's more potential with plan B," said the old man. "It doesn't rely on somebody opening the curtains."

"It's messier. Plus, we'll lose Mills. She could be an asset, sir. I'd like to try and keep her alive and out of prison."

"Okay, let it roll."

Jackson left his office and stepped into the operations room. Reg was sat at his desk watching Melody and listening to the audio traffic that was being broadcast from the tiny audio bug that Melody had planted. The audio was sent over satellite link to the operations room and was being played through the ceiling speakers. The heavy breathing of a sleeping man was slightly humorous at first, but soon it had become background noise, and Reg was able to focus on Melody. Whenever nobody was looking, he would change the tracker view from Melody to Harvey to make sure he was in position then switch back to Melody.

"Tenant," said Jackson, "how's Melody doing?"

"No change," said Reg. "Sun up in one hour."

"Okay. You know her well, right?"

"We worked together for a few years," said Reg.

"Okay, I want you to handle her," said Jackson. "We have fifteen hours until the speech, which means in twelve hours' time, if those curtains haven't opened and she hasn't taken the shot, she'll need to get herself over there to do the job manually."

"Manually?" asked Reg.

"Manually, Tenant. She'll need a plan in place before she goes. Give her the heads up so she can work on it."

"You're sending her in alone?" said a female voice from behind Jackson.

"Ladyluck, when I talk to you, you'll know it because I'll look at you."

"Sorry, sir, but, we don't even know who's in there, and it's my job to ensure the safety-"

"It's your job to sit on your arse and obey orders, Ladyluck," snapped Jackson. Then his voice softened. "I'm not going to let anything happen to her. She'll be fine. She'll formulate a plan, run it by me, and we'll help where we can."

Jackson turned back to Reg. "Tenant, you look like you want to tell me something."

"Erm, no, sir," said Reg. "I'll, err, get her onto the plan then."

Reg watched Jackson walk away and met Ladyluck's confused look. Jackson was acting out of character. Reg knew it. Ladyluck knew it. The whole room knew it.

CHAPTER FOURTEEN

"Wakey, wakey, Mrs Turvey," said Crowe. "Today's the day I've been waiting a long time for."

Angie stirred on the couch. Omar lifted his head from the dining table where he'd slept with his face buried in his arms.

"Come on, get yourself up. One way or another, today will be the last day you see your lovely husband." He smiled cruelly at the woman who was struggling to sit upright.

"I need the washroom, and I want to see my daughter," said Angie, offering no compromise. She raised her head and locked eyes with Julie's deathly gaze, who hung from her wrists with her head hanging forward.

Crowe thought about it for a moment. "Use the downstairs washroom. Omar will wake Anya when you're done."

Angie pushed off the couch to her feet and hopped across the floor to the washroom.

"Angie, darling," said Crowe. She stopped, held onto the hallway door frame, and turned to him. "Don't do anything I wouldn't do." He winked at her.

She hopped the last few steps to the washroom where she closed and locked the door before sitting down. Angie held herself together for a few moments then all her emotions came flooding out at once. With her face in her hands, she tried to stifle her sobs; she didn't want Crowe to hear her crying. But she couldn't stop. The pictures he'd shown her of Bernie and the girls had been bad enough, and she'd pretended to brush it off. But the photos of the other men in his bed were disgusting, horrifying even. It was suddenly as if she didn't know Bernie at all. She'd suspected him of cheating a few times. But she always knew he loved her and cared for her with everything he had. In some crazy way, she could understand the other girls, accept it almost, but she couldn't accept that he'd cheated on her with other men.

A part of her didn't care. A part of her just wanted him to be there to tell her it was all over, and they were going to be fine. But something gripped her heart and squeezed her chest. It pulled to remind her of the impending agony, tugging on her insides.

She thought of Anya. One way or another, her daughter was about to be heartbroken. Angie held her tummy, remembering how precious it was when Anya was inside, and how they'd sworn to protect her from the world, from bad people, people like Crowe. She had to get through this. She had to be positive and stay sharp. She'd wait for the next opportunity, and then strike, anything to delay the inevitable. Maybe if she hurt Crowe or Omar, the balance would shift. First things first, she'd get Anya in her arms and ask to have the tape removed. She couldn't do anything with her hands and feet bound.

Angie finished, pulled the chain, and then hopped out of the washroom. She leaned on the door frame and waited for Crowe to address her.

"What do you think you're doing standing there?" he asked, his tone reminiscent of an old school teacher, scolding and cold.

"I need to stretch my legs. Can you just remove the tape, please? I haven't been a problem, have I?"

Footsteps on the tiled hallway floor behind her caused Crowe to stare past Angie. She turned to find Omar coming down the stairs.

"She's gone," said Omar.

"Gone?" said Crowe in his sharp, aggressive tone. "How *can* she be gone?"

Omar lifted his hand and showed two pieces of duct tape that had been gnawed through. "She must have got out of the window."

Crowe stepped up to Angie. She turned to move away, but he struck her in the face, sending her to the floor. With her hands bound, Angie was unable to stop herself falling. Her face bounced off the hard tiles, and she felt the sharp dagger-like stab of a broken cheekbone.

"You bitch. You put her up to this, didn't you?"

Angie tried to move but was stuck laying on her bound arms. "No," she mumbled, with her face against the floor. "How could I?"

Crowe kicked her hard in the kidney then turned to Omar. "*Don't just bloody stand there*, go find her. Bring her back," he screamed.

Omar turned and left, closing the front door behind him. Crowe focused his attention on Angie once more. He reached down and grabbed a handful of hair, pulling her face from the floor.

"Get up, bitch," he snarled, and pulled harder, dragging Angie to her feet.

"You want me to remove the tape? I'll remove the tape for you." He slapped her once more, sending sharp stabs of pain into her cheek. Then he pushed her toward the back of the couch. She stumbled forward, and her elbows hung onto the leather.

Crowe bent to rip the tape at her ankles and snatched it clean off her skin with two hard tugs.

"How's that?" he asked. Then, without waiting for a reply, he kicked her legs open and put his hand on the back of her neck. "Let's see what Mr Turvey has been neglecting all these years." Crowe reached down with his free hand and raised the back of Angie's dress. "Not bad, Mrs Turvey," said Crowe.

"Get off me, you pig," said Angie, as she began to struggle against Crowe's grip.

"Now, now," he said, "don't you think you owe me a little something for my troubles? We can do this now, or we can do this when Omar brings your dirty little bitch child back here. Maybe she can watch?"

Angie kicked back and up with the heel of her foot and connected with Crowe's genitals. He doubled over behind her but maintained his grip.

"You're beginning to get on my tits, Mrs Turvey," he wheezed. "There's only one thing left for you."

He dragged her to the floor then grabbed her hair and pulled her across the smooth tiles to where Julie hung, her body already stiffening.

Crowe kicked Angie. "Get up."

Angie didn't move; she was frozen in horror.

Crowe sent a full-fisted punch to her eye and knocked her flat against the floor once more.

The harsh sound of curtains being ripped back and the slap of Crowe's open hand against her bare skin woke Angie from her unconscious state into a semi-conscious world where nothing made sense, and every part of her body hurt. Her mind span. A dull ache throbbed inside her head. A sharp pain stabbed her face and aches tugged in her tummy for Anya. She hoped Anya had gotten away and was getting help. She hoped the ordeal would soon be over. Dark dizziness overcame her, and Angie awoke with a splitting headache. Hard sunlight pierced her eyes, blinding her, but she was upright. She was tied up and hanging by her wrists. She closed her eyes and focused on the dark, turning her head away from the light. When she reopened them, she found that she'd been bound once more. She had been tied in a crucifix, naked, and face to face with Julie.

CHAPTER FIFTEEN

The room where Melody lay upon the table by the balcony doors was west facing. The sun quickly began to light the houses on the far side of the small channel of water that separated the fronds as it rose behind her. She took another look through the binos at the Turvey house and shuddered to think of what might be happening inside. A career of dealing with some of Britain's sickest minds had left her with a bad taste and a vivid imagination of what people are capable of and the lengths they will go to get their way.

She was aware that as the sun rose, she would be visible from the other houses on the opposite frond, the Turvey's neighbours. So she rolled off the table and stretched then pulled her own curtains closed, leaving enough of a gap for her to see only the Turvey house.

A sudden image of Harvey sprang to her mind as she stood by the balcony door. She paused with her hand on the curtain and thoughts of the operation slipped from her mind. How nice it would be for Harvey to be with her now, and Boon. They'd watch the glow of the sun warm the calm Arabian Gulf and light the sand coloured houses in hues of orange and yellow.

Melody took the opportunity to use the washroom then returned to resume her position on the table. She'd rolled up a blanket to lean on, which had unravelled during the long night. Pulling it off the table, she began to roll it up again, ready for round two. She stared through the gap in the curtains, her mind split between Harvey and the job in hand.

It wasn't until she was placing the rolled-up blanket on the table that her mind registered the movement she had just seen inside the floor-to-ceiling sliding doors of the Turvey house. She spun around and peered through the gap. Reaching for the binos and finding the magnified doors, she took a breath then rolled onto the table. The slightly angled view of her elevated position gave her a side image of somebody tied to the wall beside the double doors, somebody who looked to be naked and struggling. It had to be Mrs Turvey. The curtains had been opened.

Melody's heart began to race. So she took deep breaths to control the rise and drop of the scope. She flexed her fingers, blinked and readied herself for the man she'd been hunting to step into view.

The curtains blowing in the breeze that rolled off the water were the only movement Melody saw. Each time the curtains moved, she was sickened by the sight of Mrs Turvey's pink and vulnerable skin. She waited, tense and ready to strike, her finger poised over the trigger, daring not even to swallow. She focused on her small shallow breaths, in through her nose and out through pouted lips, blowing the cool air onto her fingers.

Time stood still. It was as if she were in the room with Mrs Turvey as something struck her, and her body recoiled toward the opened door as far as her restraints would allow.

Melody now knew where the man was standing. He was behind Mrs Turvey and behind the wall, out of sight.

She slowly reached up to her ear-piece without moving the

perfect positioning of the Diemaco that lay cradled in her hands, ready to wipe one more evil human off the earth.

She pushed the button on the ear-piece and held it until she heard a tiny beep which meant that the comms channel would stay open, disabling the push-to-talk function. Reg would be able to hear everything she said, and she'd hear everything he said. There was a small delay as her voice was encrypted, transmitted up to a satellite, then bounced around the earth to another satellite above London, where it was sent down to a receiver, decrypted and broadcast over the ceiling speakers as sound waves.

"Contact," she said. It was one word that woke a room of tired operatives into a heightened state of awareness. "I have eyes on Mrs Turvey."

Jackson paced across the room to the mic which sat to one side of Reg. "Mills, tell us what you see."

"The rear doors are open. The curtains are pulled back. But the only movement has been Mrs Turvey so far. No sign of any male."

"We have movement at the front of the house," said Reg. "I'm on the satellite, but I'll have to be quick before I'm discovered." There was a pause while Reg identified what he could see. "IC6 male walking to the front door. He's inside."

"He's definitely inside?" asked Jackson.

"He's gone from view," said Reg. "Mills, you should see movement any second. I need to cut the video feed."

"I'm all eyes," said Melody, slowly and quietly. She tried to keep her heart from pounding. She'd spent hours in the prone position facing targets, both wooden and human. She knew she could make the shot, but with Mrs Turvey and potentially the daughter around, there was no room for error. It would need to be a clean shot.

"Hold on," said Melody. "I see something, a leg. I have his leg. Mrs Turvey is blocking the view."

"Can she move?" asked Jackson.

"Looks like she's tied up to something. I can't see what."

The room in London went from being a hive of activity as operatives hurried to bring plans forward and ready themselves for their part in the play to dead silence, as every ear hung on the words Melody was saying.

"Damn it. He moved too quick. I have one IC1 male inside. It looks like he's talking to somebody out of sight."

"Could be the IC6?" said Jackson.

"Okay, he's moving back," said Melody.

"Description?" asked Jackson.

"Silver hair, smart, fifties."

"Crowe," said Jackson. "Take him down."

"Hold on," said Melody. "He's moving into view."

Crowe pulled the curtain back and began to step outside.

"Executing in three..."

Crowe reached outside the doors and seemed to take a breath of fresh air.

"Two."

He looked out across the water, then side to side.

"One."

Crowe quickly pulled his head back in and slid the door closed.

"Shit," said Melody.

"Mills?" said Jackson. "Take your time."

"He's gone. The door's closed."

"Tell me you're kidding."

"No, he just came out to close the door."

"You missed your chance, Mills," said Jackson. "I thought you said you could handle this?"

"With all due respect, I don't see you out here."

"Stop right there, Mills."

"I'll stop when I want to stop. Right now, I'm about to send a 7.62 round across the water at eight hundred metres per second, and I have inches to spare before I kill your boss' wife, and God knows, maybe his daughter too. So I'll take my sweet time, and make sure I get it right, sir." She closed off with finality.

"That's it, Mills, you let it out," said Jackson, smiling. "How do you feel?"

"With all due respect, Jackson, keep your mouth shut and let me run the play. I'm here, you're not."

"Anything you say, Mills," said Jackson, calmly and strangely pleased with her outburst.

"Hold on," said Melody. "I see movement."

"Tenant, get that screen up, satellite."

"Okay, but you have a thirty-second window before they trace it," said Reg in a playful warning tone.

"Just get it up," said Jackson.

"Oh, Christ," said Melody.

"Mills, talk to me," said Jackson.

"It's the little girl," said Melody. "She's standing right outside the doors."

CHAPTER SIXTEEN

The sound of a magazine slotting into a SIG handgun, followed by the smooth action of the weapon being armed and a round sliding into place was a familiar sound to Harvey, especially when it was done with the speed and control of an expert weapons handler like Melody. It was a sound he hadn't heard for a long time, yet would somehow never forget.

He'd heard Melody's last words and was himself staring at the little girl stood innocently at the French doors. He was unable to move until he heard the doors crash open and Melody's boots squeak across the tiled floor and out of earshot. There was no way Harvey would get across the water before her if he leapt from the balcony. In fact, even as he stood to enter the room, he saw her bound down the stairs beside the pool onto the beach. She sprinted across the sand, took two large steps into the water, and dove in.

Harvey watched as she reappeared twenty-seconds later halfway across the channel. He moved inside and lay himself down on the table.

By the time Harvey made himself comfortable and found Melody in the rifle's telescopic scope, she was striding out of the water. The little girl stood at the glass doors, unseen by Crowe and Omar. She turned in response to Melody calling her, but then quickly turned back and peered in through the glass.

Melody bounded up the steps into the Turvey's rear garden. She crossed the small lawn and was just metres away from picking the little girl up in a swoop when the doors suddenly slid open. But nobody appeared. Harvey couldn't see the figure who had opened the doors, but his finger felt for the trigger. Melody had frozen. She crouched down to the girl and stroked her hair. Melody was talking to someone inside the house, someone out of Harvey's sight. Harvey kept his focus on the open doors. He could see pale skin, and the unmistakable form of a woman struggling against restraints, the mother, he guessed.

Harvey could see how unwavering Melody was even from the distance he was at. She kept control as much as she could. But it wasn't until the handgun pointed out from the open door that Harvey knew she was no longer in control. She was in serious trouble.

The gun was followed by an arm. It had tanned skin but not like the glowing tan on a westerner, so Harvey wondered if it belonged to a local. Then a shoulder appeared. From this range, Harvey's chances of hitting an arm were slim. He'd need the head. The torso would be better, but a head might be doable.

Harvey ran through the checklist Melody had taught him. He remembered her words. *"Even in the tensest moments, when the target is speeding by, the checklist must be complete before you pull the trigger. That's the only way you'll know for sure that you gave it all you had."*

A glance with his free eye caught the large flat leaves of the palm trees outside, barely moving. The water was still. The rifle was loaded, safety off. The butt of the weapon was firmly pressed into his shoulder. His eye was a good three inches behind the scope. His breathing was checked.

Melody stood with her hand on the head of the girl.

"Move, damn it," whispered Harvey.

She was blocking his view. Harvey remained focused on the arm and shoulder, waiting for the torso or head to step into his cross-hairs.

His breathing increased, and he checked it with three long, deep breaths. Melody moved again, directly in his field of vision. The small cross in his scope planted firmly on the back of Melody's head. He daren't move but he eased his finger away from the trigger. He knew Melody liked a hair trigger. Barely a strong a breeze would be enough to bring the hammer down.

And then, in a moment of coordinated synchronicity and luck, the arm became a shoulder then a face, and Melody reached down to protect the girl.

Harvey fired.

CHAPTER SEVENTEEN

Angie didn't hear the shot. She only saw the chaos that ensued.

Before the shot, she saw Anya suddenly at the door looking scared. Her eyes were bright red, and she had scratches down her bare legs. Angie had tried to shoo her away, to get her to run, to find somebody. But the little girl had just stood there confused as to why her mummy wasn't opening the doors to pick her up. Angie had mouthed for her to run away, get help, but the scared eight-year-old girl had been too afraid to move. She hadn't budged.

Then there had been a woman. She was wet as if she'd come from the sea. Angie had been momentarily filled with hope, a sudden moment of heart-lifting joy that had been cut down when Omar too had seen the movement. He'd stepped up to the sliding doors, hidden behind the curtain, and waited for the woman to get close to Anya. Then he'd snatched the door open and aimed his gun outside. Anya had cried for her mum, loud and shrill. Omar had shouted for the woman to get down on the ground. The woman had shouted back insults at Omar. All the while, Crowe had stood out of the way beside Angie, smiling as the events unfolded.

Crowe pulled a handgun from his waistband and quietly put it against Angie's head. Angie immediately froze, scared to move a muscle. The feeling of the hard steel against her temple and knowing a bullet was inside just waiting to end her life was terrifying. She wasn't afraid of the pain. She wasn't afraid of dying. But she *was* afraid for Anya.

Then, without warning, Omar had flinched as if he'd seen something behind the stranger. The woman had bent to grab Anya, and the back of Omar's head cracked open. Blood spattered across Angie's face, the floor and the walls. His body slumped the ground, half in and half out of their holiday home.

"Mrs Turvey, are you okay?" said the woman. "I can't see you. Are you hurt?"

"Mummy," screamed Anya.

"Don't say a word," whispered Crowe in her ear.

"Mrs Turvey, talk to me," came the woman's voice again.

"One false move, bitch," said Crowe, "and they both get it."

Angie heard the woman talking to Anya from behind the wall. "Stay here, okay? Do not move." There was a pause and the racking of a weapon. Angie recognised the sound from movies. "I'm coming inside. I know you're there, Angie. Trust me. Everything's going to be okay."

A booted female foot stepped onto the tiled floor.

"That's far enough," said Crowe.

The woman stopped.

"Let her go, Crowe, this isn't worth it."

"Drop the gun."

"Crowe, let's talk about this. You're surrounded. There's armed police all around you."

"There'll be one less if you don't drop that weapon," said Crowe confidently.

The woman threw the gun onto the couch.

"Good. Now step inside and bring the girl."

"You don't need her. Let her go," said the stranger.

Crowe laughed. "And let her run to the police? You should have done your homework, missy. You clearly have no idea who I am."

"I know who you are. You're Caesar Crowe. You're a criminal whose career is about to come to a grinding halt."

"Stop stalling. Get inside and bring the girl."

Angie watched as the woman bent down to pick up Anya.

"I'm watching you," said Crowe.

"I was just picking up the girl. You can't expect her to walk over-"

"Over what?"

The stranger looked at the floor where Omar's body was slumped.

"Oh, I see," said Crowe. "Yes, that might be a little disturbing for her. Close the door."

Angie made eye contact with her daughter, who looked up expecting to be hugged. But Angie couldn't move.

"Well this is fun, isn't it?" said Crowe. "The four of us. How about you new girls take a seat?"

The stranger didn't move, but Anya hugged her leg and hid her face from Crowe.

"It wasn't an offer," said Crowe. "*Sit down.*"

"Why don't you let Angie go, or at least let her get dressed?"

"Why don't you do as you're told and sit down?"

"Maybe I don't want to sit," said the woman.

"Oh, you'll sit. Even if I have to break your legs, you'll sit. Who are you anyway? And what are you doing here? Who sent you? Was it *Bernie*?"

"Bernie who?"

"Don't play games with me. I'm smarter than the average bear."

"Oh, you're smart, Crowe. I have no doubt about that. But

smart isn't going to stop you from being tossed in a cell to live out the rest of your sorry life."

"Who says it's going to come to that?" replied Crowe. "MI6 send a whining little bitch to stop me. Is that it? Is that all they think of me?"

"MI who?" asked the stranger.

"Don't play games. I won't tell you again. I know it was MI6 that sent you. But maybe they sent *you* because you're not a real operative. I'm right, aren't I? They can't operate here, it would get all..." Crowe gestured with crazy hands, waving his gun around. "Political. Am I right? So they sent you. Probably some little upstart with a smart mouth and knows exactly what to do with it. Hmm?"

"You're wrong, Crowe."

"I'm wrong, am I? About what? You having a smart mouth or you being keen to get up the ladder?"

Crowe moved away from Angie and strode over to the woman, who moved Anya behind her out of his reach.

"I bet you banged your way from office to office, licked your way through your exams, and rode the promotion pole until you could fuck no further?" He sniffed at Melody like an elderly man might enjoy the scent of a wild flower. "Well, I have news for you, little lady." Crowe walked behind her, and Anya moved around to her front, then he softly whispered in the stranger's ear. "This is the end of the ride for you." The woman tensed and Angie guessed Crowe had the gun in the small of her back.

"Put the gun down," said the stranger. "No pads, just you and me. We'll see whose end is coming."

"Not long now until we all have a little face to face with our friends in England, ten hours and fifteen minutes to be precise. During that ten hours, you have two choices. You can make life hard and die painfully. Or you can sit down, be good, and pray that Mr Turvey completes his end of the bargain."

She walked away from him towards the sofa, taking Anya with her, and disappeared from Angie's view.

Angie heard the duct tape being ripped from its roll. Four times, she heard the screech of tape being pulled out then the rip. Angie knew it meant that both Anya and the woman had their wrists and ankles bound. Now they were all prisoners. Crowe walked to the sliding doors, pulled Omar's body inside by his belt, slammed the door and snatched the curtain closed once more. For a brief moment, he was exposed to whoever took Omar down and Melody waited for the shot. But the moment had been too fleeting.

"Nothing like a little privacy, Angie. Now, where were we before we were so pleasantly interrupted?"

CHAPTER EIGHTEEN

"Oh my God, sir, we need to get her out of there," said Lady-luck. The rest of the room sat horrified at what they'd just heard over the comms. "She had no business going inside. And did I hear right, someone just got shot?"

"The time for your opinion is not now, Ladyluck. We'd all appreciate it if you kept it to yourself for the foreseeable future. Now is the time for planning, and taking down Crowe." Jackson turned to Reg. "Tenant, how are we doing with the live feed?"

"Which one, sir?" said Reg. "The house or the charity gig?"

"Mr Turvey's speech. We need to make sure that we have control over the live feed. We can't have a live suicide all over the media."

"You think he'll go through with it, sir?" asked Reg.

Jackson gave the question consideration. "What would you do if the two people you loved the most had a gun to their heads and all you had to do to save them was to pull the trigger yourself?"

"Hard to say, sir. How do you even try to empathise?" replied Reg.

"All we can do is communicate, and work as hard as we

damn well can to bring Crowe down, preferably before Turvey takes the mic."

Reg opened his mouth to say something, but stopped, and turned away.

"Tenant? What is it?" asked Jackson. "You've been acting funny for a few hours now. If there's something you think I should know then now would be a great time to say so."

Reg turned his head back. "It's just that Melody is a friend. I feel like we're not doing everything we can to help her. Surely the Dubai government can send in their boys?"

"Okay. So do you want to call the Prime Minister, wake him up, and ask him to get on the blower to his counterpart in Dubai? Can you imagine how that call would go, Tenant? First of all, the fact that we even have operatives over there goes against the treaty that somebody far more intelligent than ourselves dreamed up and worked hard to get put in place. Secondly, if we send in troops, either our own or the UAE's, Crowe will terminate Mrs Turvey and the kid. We have our hands tied, Tenant. Whatever we do, we need to be smart and it needs to be covert, and van loads of blokes with automatic weapons are not covert. I need you switched on, Tenant. Are you switched on?"

Reg nodded slowly. "Yeah. Yeah, I'm switched on."

"Good," said Jackson. "Don't worry, we'll get her out."

Jackson left the room, and Reg opened a discreet chat window with Harvey. He typed out a message that read, '*M has been caught. She's being held with the mother and daughter. Clock is ticking. Options are minimal.*' Then before he hit send, he deleted the long message, looked around once more to make sure nobody was watching his screen, then simply typed, '*M is in trouble.*'

CHAPTER NINETEEN

The scope of the Diemaco gave Harvey a clear view of Melody bending down to pick up the girl then stepping inside the house. He saw her toss her weapon. He still had no idea of how many men were in there, or how much danger she was in. Harvey knew that Melody could handle herself. They sparred frequently, and although Harvey usually came out on top, Melody was a tenacious fighter who rarely backed down.

He knew Melody would be wondering who took the shot. Harvey had no idea if other operatives were waiting for a signal or prepared to step in. A calm disposition was one of Harvey's many traits. The ability to keep a cool composure when the pressure was on was key to staying alive in many cases. He thought back to his training as he always did, when his mentor, Julios, had taught him the three steps to a successful mission. Patience, planning and execution.

Aware of his own abilities, Harvey had a good idea that he could steam into the house, take out whoever was holding Melody, and get them both out alive. He couldn't however, be so sure about collateral. Melody was trained and would act as soon as she saw her chance. But somebody untrained, like the little girl, would likely be hurt or killed in the attempt. Harvey remained still. He lay prone on the table Melody had set up, with the curtains drawn, leaving just a small gap for him to keep an eye on the house.

Two plans formulated in Harvey's mind. Whatever was occurring in the house had the pressure of time. Pressure meant mistakes. He'd wait for that mistake and be ready to act. Plan B was for when plan A had run out of time. He studied the house, and like all the other villas, it had a flat roof with air conditioning units and water tanks. The climb up would be easy, as he could walk carefully along the pergola, and up the maintenance ladder that was fixed to the side of the house. There was space for him to move about on the roof and, given the chance, he could drop down onto the second-floor balcony. If the house across the water had similar windows to the house he was in, Harvey would be inside within seconds. From there, he could take whoever it was by surprise.

He made the decision to stick with plan A until nightfall, then plan B would come into play.

A small vibration in his pocket signalled an incoming message. He pulled his phone out and saw the screen displayed a little silhouette of a cartoon spy that Reg had created to differentiate alerts from the LUCY app from other apps. The alert simply read, "*M is in trouble.*"

Harvey didn't reply.

He lay still, almost catatonic. His arms were locked, so the weight of the rifle wasn't pulling on his muscles. He could be ready to fire at a moment's notice. But as ready as he was to take the shot, he knew deep down that as the sun sank lower in the sky and the red and orange hues of warm light washed over the house, he would be leaving soon and pushing plan B into action. Shadows of palms grew long across the water until they eventually merged with the blackness of the sea. Lights from nearby houses cast an unnatural glow over areas of the beach but left strips of shadow between the structures. Harvey made the weapon safe, laid it down, and rolled off the table.

Harvey had decided he wouldn't swim the channel, he would run around it. It would take longer and be much further. But for what he had to do, being wet would be a hindrance.

The run took a little under twenty minutes. Again, Harvey ran in the soft wet sand near the shore so the incoming tide would cover his tracks. The whole time he was running, he thought about Melody. Harvey considered this fact: he'd never really been in love before. He guessed it was love, although he had no comparison. But he also didn't like being without her. He couldn't imagine life without her. He liked the feeling. Although it came with its own set of vulnerabilities, it felt right. The timing was good; maybe settling down and letting Melody have a career of her own wasn't such a bad thing. He could still do the things he wanted to do. Of course, he'd worry, just like thousands if not millions of other husbands and wives around the world who worried about their spouses when they went to work. Firemen, policemen, soldiers. Melody and Harvey would be no different. Maybe he could just keep an eye on her. Maybe that would be his way of staying sane.

Harvey stopped a few houses down from the large villa that Melody had disappeared inside. Standing on the edge of the beach, he pushed all thoughts of Melody and their future behind him and basked in the shadows, allowing his senses to take stock of the situation.

A few small fish splashed in the water nearby. Larger predator fish were chasing them, maybe. Heavy palm leaves scraped against neighbouring leaves in the gentle breeze. But nothing else moved. He studied the rear of the house. Traces of light outlined the rear sliding doors, but the rest of the house was dark. Above the doors, a small red LED blinked, a movement sensor. Harvey checked the house next door where there was no blinking LED and the lights were all out. His plan adjusted.

Making his way through the rear garden of the adjacent house, he reached up to the top of the wall that adjoined the Turvey house and pulled himself quietly up. The pergola, a wooden structure designed to provide shade, was just a few steps away along the wall. Its thick wooden beams took his weight easily.

Once on the Turvey property, Harvey worked his way toward the roof access ladder, which was fixed to the side of the house.

The steel rungs were cool to the touch and wet from the humidity of the night. A short while later, Harvey was on the Turvey's flat roof, ducked down behind one of the four air conditioning units that stood near each corner.

He waited a full minute before making his next move. The standard minute was longer than most people had the patience to wait. If he'd been heard during his climb, the standard minute wait was long enough for anyone looking to give up and put the noises down to an animal or a bird.

The first-floor balcony was a fifteen-foot drop from the roof. It had looked less through the scope of the rifle, but it was still doable. Harvey lowered himself down. He guessed his feet were still roughly seven or eight feet from the balcony, but just four feet from the balustraded handrail that ran around the edge. He twisted his body to see his feet below, then hung from one hand. Then let go. His feet found the wide stone handrail easily. He bent his knees to absorb his weight and flung his arms out to balance. Straightening, he checked his surroundings once more and dropped to the floor.

A hard look at the glass door on the balcony told him the curtains were open, but the lights were off. It was too early for people to be sleeping, so the room should be empty. If it wasn't, he'd need to use plan C, extreme violence and a controlled chaos of attacks on the men. It was a last resort and one that did not guarantee success.

Harvey was unarmed. He was going up against an unknown number of men who must be armed, else Melody would not have given her own weapon up so easily. He just didn't know what they were armed with. His first priority would be to clear the top floor. He tried the door handle slowly and gently and felt the resistance of the locking mechanism. Giving a little extra effort, the handle moved more until it clicked open. Presumably, it had been overlooked, deemed secure due to its height.

The room was silent and dark. There were no sounds of breathing, no sign of movement. He was alone. The bedroom door was open, so he carefully moved closer and peered around the corner. It was cool from the air conditioning and the stairway at the far end of the tiled hallway was partially lit from the lighting downstairs. Harvey considered how he'd manage a hostage situation in this house. If he had help, he'd have the hostages locked in a bedroom with a guard. But all the bedroom doors were open with no lights on. So if everybody was downstairs, perhaps that meant that the number of men controlling the situation was small, possibly just one or two. One or two men with at least three hostages meant that Melody and her fellow prisoners would likely be tied up.

He stepped out into the hallway and stood at the top of the stairs, listening, breathing, absorbing the atmosphere. He waited a full minute before he stepped onto the top stair and then heard footsteps on the tiled floor downstairs. Pulling back, he glanced at his escape route, a dark bedroom adjacent to the stairway.

A man appeared in the downstairs hallway. Harvey saw only the back of the man, grey-haired, dressed neatly, and not ready for any combat in brogues and suit pants. The man opened a door. Harvey judged it to be the inner entrance to the garage. It was to the front of the house beside, what looked to be, the main front doors. A jingle of keys a few seconds later confirmed Harvey's suspicions.

The man returned, closed the garage door and strode back to the rear of the house. Harvey began to get a feel for the layout of the building; all the activity seemed to be at the back. Again, he considered what he would do. He would have a man at the front, near the window, to raise the alarm should an armed response unit close in.

The vibration of his phone in his thigh pocket caused him to stop. He couldn't risk reading the message now. It could only be from Reg. Lighting up his phone might catch the eye of somebody, a reflection or a shadow. It could wait.

Harvey crept silently down the sweeping staircase, all the time alert for any changes in sound from below. He was two steps from the bottom when he caught a narrow glimpse through the rear of the house. Two women were tied to the wall. Both naked. One was clearly dead. Harvey had seen enough death to know that a human body lost its natural sheen and colour after a day. The second woman was either asleep or had recently been killed. Her skin was alive and bore red patchy slap marks.

Another step.

The body of the man he'd killed lay on the floor behind a couch in a small pool of blood. Harvey could only see the back of the seat as it faced away from him. Why hadn't they moved the body away to another room, or outside? Again, with few men to watch the prisoners, they wouldn't have that luxury; the body would have to stay there.

Harvey could see through to the curtains that had shielded the rear doors. The room opened up to the right and to the left, out of his sight. If there were couches to the right, perhaps the area on the left was a dining area. He was in full view now, and anyone who walked into the hallway would see him. The kitchen was halfway along the hallway. Harvey hoped for a wooden block of sharp kitchen knives, maybe even a carelessly stored gun. But a knife would suffice. If he acted fast, he knew he could take down two or three armed men with just a knife given the right circumstances, circumstances that he'd have to instigate.

Harvey took the last step.

It was then he heard Melody's whisper.

"How do you plan on getting out of here alive?"

CHAPTER TWENTY

"I presume by your aggressive posture, and the fact you didn't even knock before entering, that Mills is now a prisoner inside the Turvey house and that Stone is somewhere close by ready to land himself in hot water," said the old man in his reclining leather office chair.

"Correct, sir."

"And you're mad at me for putting her in this situation?"

"I'm annoyed that you put *me* in this situation, sir," said Jackson. "We now have another hostage and a potential political nightmare on our hands and all because you want Stone out of the picture."

"I don't want Stone out of the picture, Jackson. I want him out of every picture. He's wild, he knows too much, and besides," said the old man lazily, "he's a lunatic, a torturer. He needs to go."

"There are other ways of achieving that without endangering the lives of good people and my career."

"So you're doubting me? You're scared. I'm beginning to question if I chose the right man for this job, Jackson. Do you want to step down? Because I can tell you now, it's a big step and an awful long drop. Keep talking like you're talking and no-one will even hear you hit the floor. Do you understand what I'm saying, Jackson?"

"I know what's right and wrong, sir," said Jackson.

"You said yourself that Stone needs locking up. He only got away last time because Mills tricked you. That tells me two things. Mills is good, possibly smarter than you, but Stone is better and definitely smarter than you. Right now, we have three hostages, including Mills, and we have an unofficial but extremely capable asset on the ground, who is not about to let the love of his life die in some feeble hostage attempt. Mills will be okay. Even if she's locked up, we can get her out. Stone will either be shot dead by Dubai police when our asset calls it in, or he'll spend the rest of his life sharing a cell and a bucket with twenty other guys in the middle of the desert. Turvey dies. You and I both move up the ladder. We both get rewarded for averting a political nightmare, and all you have to do is keep your mouth shut, and do what I tell you."

The old man reached for the bottom drawer of his desk and pulled out two tumblers and a small bottle of brandy.

"You have it all planned out, don't you? But you never told me why you want Stone so badly anyway." said Jackson.

The old man finished pouring two healthy measures of brandy. He twisted the cap on and left the bottle on the desk.

"You don't get to sit in this seat without having a few things in place." He passed Jackson the second glass and took a sip from his own. His tongue ran around his lips, savouring the bitter flavour. "First of all, you need to know people. It's a gener-ation thing. Age and maturity tend to instil a little more confi-dence in people. You make new friends. You learn things. One of the things you learn fastest is who you can and can't trust. Stone and Mills were assigned to an old friend of mine, Frank Carver. Tenant was on the team too. Now *he's* an intelligent guy. But *not one* of them ever questioned Carver's integrity. Not one of them ever did a background check on him. It took a full internal investigation with MI5, and yourself, to catch him."

He took another long sip of the brandy and continued.

"No doubt, if Tenant had thought to run a background check on Carver, he'd have seen that Carver and I go way back. We started out together. We were often up against each other for promotions, and we ended up having a healthy respect for each other's skills, tenacity and ability to minimise risk." The old man smiled. "Risk management, Jackson. You need to be able to identify risk and eliminate it. Right now, we have a lunatic out there who knows too much about Carver. And if he knows too much about Carver-"

"Then he knows too much about you," finished Jackson.

"That's the way it all works. That's a risk. Do you understand?"

"You're covering your own backside."

"I'm eliminating risk. Understood?"

"However you want to word it, you're just getting even because you think Stone killed your friend. Now you're worried because you were also up to no good." Jackson paused. "But yeah, I get it."

"Good. Now go eliminate Stone."

CHAPTER TWENTY-ONE

Jackson walked into the ops room. His team were all hard at work finding a hole in Crowe's plan, searching for allies who could step in without publicising the operation, and formulating plans. The tension was electric; the stakes were high. The operation was close to home; it was personal, and the team were throwing everything they had at stopping it.

The effort was apparent. Even at a glance, Jackson could see how determined people were. It made him proud. Jackson himself had handpicked a lot of the team when he'd made the move from MI5 to MI6, and his decisions were now bearing fruit. Even Ladyluck, who could be emotional, brash, and sensitive, was pulling out all the stops only to hit the same walls as the rest of the team. But she kept going, undeterred.

Jackson took the spare seat next to Tenant and watched as the tech guru's fingers danced across the keyboard. Tenant wore large headphones, had his feet on a cushioned stool under his desk and stared up at the screens in front of him. Jackson was about to tap him on the shoulder when the door opened. Framed by the harsh corridor lights was Bernard Turvey.

Jackson stared at the shell of his boss. Turvey's strong exterior mask couldn't hide the pain and sleepless nights in his eyes, nor the slump in shoulders.

"Team," said Jackson, alerting them of Turvey's presence.

Slowly, keyboards stopped tapping, mice stopped clicking, and all heads turned to the man at the door.

An uneasy silence filled the room like a noxious gas. It stopped everyone in their tracks. Whatever they were thinking about was snatched from their minds. Bernard Turvey's life and death, and the choice he had to make, filled the void in their heads.

Bernard looked around the room. He swallowed frequently, fighting to maintain his composure. Finally, he stepped inside and let the door swing shut behind him.

Jackson broke the silence.

"Take a seat, sir."

Turvey smiled weakly, but held his hand up, indicating he was okay.

Bernard cleared his throat. "Looking at you all in here makes me proud," he began, "prouder than any of you will ever know." His steely resistance to breaking was clear. The team looked on with admiration at the strength of the man who stood before them. His leg shook uncontrollably, yet he didn't try to hide it. His lower jaw wobbled the moment it unhinged itself from the safety of its upper counterpart, yet the man continued to speak, unashamed and resolute. His wet and shiny eyes shone from the glow of the computer screens in the relative darkness of the room.

"You all have fine careers ahead of you," continued Bernard. "You are *all* at the top of your games, the peak of your abilities. And long may those abilities run free as you all continue to defy possibilities and stretch the boundaries of British intelligence and security on a daily basis."

Bernard looked around the room. He held the admiring

stares of each and every person in the room then stopped on Jackson.

"No doubt that all of you have something to say, questions to ask, feelings you want to convey. I know you do. Many of us have gotten to know each other very well, that's what comes of being surrounded by extremely capable people, and achieving incredible things together. I only wish I had the time to talk to you and to get to know you all a little better."

Bernard began to pace the room, walking alongside everyone and offering them all their own smiles in return for unsaid goodbyes. Bernard put his hand on Ladyluck's head as she broke, unable to hold her tears anymore. Angela Finsbury, the research assistant who sat beside her, put her hand on her back and rubbed gently. They spoke no words; there was nothing to say.

"What I am about to do, the decision I have made, although it seems difficult and it's hard for many of you to empathise, is the easiest decision I've ever had to make. The lives of my wife and daughter carry far more weight in the world than my own. I know I'll be remembered well, and I'll die knowing that they will live on. It'll be hard for them at first, but Anya will grow to be strong, knowing that I'm watching over her."

He paused as he completed a full circle of the room. "The truth is that, while you see it as a decision, I see only one choice. I couldn't go on living knowing that my cowardice killed the two most important people in my world. And that's the truth."

The door opened and a man wearing a suit and an ear-piece leaned in. One hand held the breast of his jacket closed, a habit formed from years of armed security. "Sir," he said in a strong, confident, Mancunian accent, "it's time."

"I'll be right out," replied Turvey. Then, as he held the door open, he paused. He turned back to face Jackson. The door seemed to be all that held him upright. "Get them out, Jackson.

Make them safe." Then he nodded his final goodbye and left the room.

The room sat stunned by the unexpected and heart-warming speech. Ladyluck cried into her sleeve. Jackson caught the attention of Angela Finsbury who was consoling Ladyluck and gestured with his head to take her to the washrooms.

"Alright, people, you know what we need to do. We have one hour before Bernard's speech. The strategy is changing. We need options on how to control this." He paused and thought about his next words carefully. "Stopping it may no longer be an option, and if that's the case, we need to control it."

Jackson turned to Tenant, who had removed his head-phones and put his feet down, but still frantically attacked his keyboard and flicked his head from screen to screen.

"Tenant," said Jackson, "where are we?"

"I have a way into the building's internet-leased line, so should the worst-case scenario look inevitable, I can cut the line. We have men on the ground ensuring that the media aren't using their own connections, and we have a high-frequency signal jammer in place just in case somebody tries. There's an armed guard on all the hotel entrances, and a third party has been brought in alongside uniformed police to handle the collection of mobile phones and tablets."

"Must be quite a scene?" said Jackson.

"It's all covert, sir. All the audience will know is that they had their mobile phone taken from them. And given that the board comprises of several MP's, I doubt they'll regard that as anything but additional security."

"Good," said Jackson, nodding. "Now talk to me about Stone."

Reg's fingers stopped dancing. His eyes stopped flicking from screen to screen. "Sir?"

"Don't kid a kidder, Tenant. What's his location?" said Jackson in a hushed tone.

"I'm not sure I know-"

"Tenant, last chance, we don't have much time," said Jackson. "I know you got him out there, but right now, we need him. Get a message to him. Can you do that?"

"Sure," said Reg, with a surprised yet ashamed expression. "What do you want me to tell him?"

"Tell him..." Jackson pondered briefly. "Tell him Jackson said to go get his girl out. Tell him to do whatever it takes to get Melody and the Turveys out of there."

"Are you okay, sir?" asked Jackson.

Jackson waited as if doubting his own thoughts. "Yeah. Yeah, I'm fine, Tenant. I just had a moment of clarity."

"Clarity, sir?"

"Also tell him..." Jackson looked over at the old man's office door hesitantly. "Also tell him to get out of there as soon as possible when it's done."

Reg looked up at him, surprised. "Jackson?"

Jackson sighed, shook his head and looked back at Reg. "Just trust me on this one, okay?"

CHAPTER TWENTY-TWO

"Melody, I know you can't respond. But you should know that we're all here for you," said Reg over the comms. His crackled and faint voice came over Melody's ear-piece. Somehow, his soft tone carried with it despite the poor connection. "Listen, we're running out of time but we're pulling out all the stops. You should see the guys here, I've never seen them so invested. What I'm trying to say, Melody, is, well, don't feel alone. No matter how hard it is, no matter what Crowe is saying or doing, we're with you, and we're coming for you." The connection dropped until Reg began speaking again. "We do need help though, Melody. Do what you can. Don't take any more risks, you've done enough. But if you can, try and get him to talk. There must be something we're missing. He's too confident. It's like he knows something we don't. See if you can bridge that gap."

Melody looked around the room. Exhaustion had overcome Angie Turvey, and she hung from her wrists, her head resting on the dead woman's head. Anya slept the deep sleep that only children seem to enjoy. Crowe sat at the dining table working on the laptop.

"How do you plan on getting out of here alive?" whispered Melody. "You know you're surrounded. So what's the plan?"

"Like I said before," began Crowe, "I'm smarter than the average bear."

"You think you're going to walk out of here? You saw what happened to your friend. You won't get two steps. There's a sniper over the water and there are snipers out front."

"I'm quite certain the British government won't be taking me down, not on Emirati soil anyway. I like my chances."

"How about a wager?" said Melody. "To give the girls a chance?"

Crowe laughed. It was an honest laugh. Not feigned, not cruel, it was genuine.

Melody continued to stare at him. "*I* bet Turvey doesn't pull the trigger," she said.

Crowe raised an eyebrow. "What's at stake here?"

"If he doesn't pull the trigger, you release the woman and the girl. Shoot me instead. Bernard doesn't have to know. He'll either do it or he won't, but that little girl and her mother have no part in this. I'm ready. Are you, Crowe?"

"It's not enough. What do I stand to win if I'm right and Turvey goes through with it?"

"What do you need?" asked Melody.

"Nothing, not from you anyway."

"Are you sure about that? I'm a resourceful girl with all sorts of things up my sleeve. You want weapons? You want a passport?"

"No way. It's not going to happen," said Crowe. But Melody caught the intrigue in his eyes.

"If I'm right," said Melody, "and Turvey doesn't kill himself, you let the girls go, and I get you out of here no questions asked. If I'm wrong, well, you do what you have to do. But right now, you don't have anywhere to go from here, and you can't stay here forever."

"I don't need your help, young lady. If he doesn't pull the trigger, his family are dead. What would *you* do? He doesn't have options."

"So you kill his family. Great. Then what? You just stroll out of here and into the arms of waiting police. They still have the death penalty here you know?"

"Young lady, do you honestly think I haven't thought of that? Do I look like the type of man to go into something like this blind? No, I do not."

"So what then?" asked Melody, "Your options are slim, and the boys outside will pull the trigger and ask questions later."

"Turvey dies. If it's not during his speech, his family dies. After that, he gets one more chance. One more chance to save lives, missy. I imagine by then he'll want to join his family anyway."

"And then what? You're out here. Do you have men in London? Is that it? If he doesn't do it, you send them in to do your dirty work?"

"Turvey is a man of many faces. I tried to tell his poor wife over there. But would she listen? Oh no. Sure, he loves his family, and he's done well. But do you know what he's had to do to get there? I'll tell you what he did. He tore my family to pieces. He killed my wife and daughter to get at me and still failed. I'm still here, and they're not. So as for your little bet, as tempting as it is, they die."

"You didn't answer the question," said Melody. "What then?"

"He's bent, as crooked as they come, in fact, in more ways than one. But one thing I do know is that he's patriotic."

"So what? Being patriotic won't help him here."

"No, you're right, it won't. But it helps me."

"How?" asked Melody.

"Let's just say that it's a matter of understanding politics over the value of a human being."

"Politics? Really, you're doing this in the name of politics? There are easier ways. Hold a sign up outside parliament or something."

"Do you know how delicate relationships are between nations right now?"

"Relationships are always delicate."

"Ah, you talk from experience," said Crowe.

"I've dabbled."

"You got burned?"

"I learned a lot," replied Melody.

"Would you do it again?"

"In a heartbeat."

"Why do think you were sent out here?"

"Who do you think is waiting for you to step outside?" said Melody.

"Nobody probably," said Crowe. "You see, if the Dubai government found out about you, not only would you be shot for espionage, but the UAE would undoubtedly sever ties with the UK. That would have a huge effect on oil and energy in the UK. And well, let's face it, where else are us Brits going to land our planes around here? It's the friendliest place for miles. If the UAE severed ties with the UK, then so would Saudi. And if that happens, then who would want to be friends with the UK? We have nothing to offer. It would be a political nightmare which would likely destroy the economy, and one the British government aren't keen to risk."

"So?" said Melody. "What's your point?"

"Well, missy, what do you think would happen with that very delicate relationship between the UAE and the UK if a bomb were to detonate, say in a mall or somewhere public?"

Melody's eyes widened.

"Or maybe if someone very important was killed in the blast?"

Melody struggled against her bindings, trying to force herself free.

Crowe smiled at her struggle. He leaned forward to face her. "Now what do you think would happen if that bomb were to be planted by a British undercover operative?"

CHAPTER TWENTY-THREE

"Listen up," said Jackson. "This just got very real."

The team all looked up from their stations.

"We have new intel, a bomb, somewhere public, possibly even targeting the Sheik's family. Ladyluck, get onto our assets. We need to know every known movement of anybody worth targeting. Finsbury, find Tenant a list of every possible public location worth bombing and tie it in with whatever Ladyluck finds. We need a crossover. Tenant, you can't do this alone. I need as many eyes as possible on every CCTV camera in whatever location Ladyluck and Finsbury come up with. Gordon, I need comms plans. If this goes south, we need to be able to pre-warn those upstairs of what is happening, and we need to be able to get a message to the British embassies in Dubai and Abu Dhabi."

"You're still keeping this under wraps?" asked Gordon.

Jackson stared at him from across the room. "I don't see what choice we have, Gordon. If we raise the alarm now, we'll be ordered to cut our losses. We'll lose Mills and the entire Turvey family."

"It's a huge risk for one family and an operative that no

longer operates," replied Gordon. "If that bomb goes off, the Turveys will be the last thing on our minds. It would destroy everything the UK stands for, sir."

Jackson took a deep breath and nodded. "You're right, but we need to give them every chance we can."

"Sir, I have eyes on Turvey," said Reg. "He's inside the hotel."

"Is he carrying?" asked Ladyluck.

"The weapon is taped to the underside of his seat. We had someone on the crew take care of it," said Jackson. "Tenant, make sure you hit that kill switch on the internet line."

"It's all ready to go, sir," replied Reg.

Jackson took a step closer to him. "Any news?"

"No response, but he's close. See this icon here?" Reg pointed discreetly to a red dot on a map displayed on one of his screens.

"That's Stone?" asked Jackson.

"Yep. Judging by the difference in signal strengths, he's on the roof or upper floor, and Melody is inside. See how weak her signal is."

"Can we talk to him?"

"No, he didn't get the standard issue ear-piece."

Jackson checked his watch. "We have thirty minutes before the speeches start."

"How long is his speech?" asked Reg.

Jackson frowned at him. "Not long enough, Tenant."

CHAPTER TWENTY-FOUR

"Ladies and gentlemen, welcome to the DWC's forty-fifth annual gala dinner," began the Master of Ceremonies. He was stood in a black tuxedo on a small stage with a decorated wooden lectern, from which a single microphone protruded. "I'm sure you're all keen to sample the wonderful meal that has been prepared for you. But if I may, I'd like to let you all know the order of events for the evening, so you can all plan your getaways." The crowd offered a weak mumble of humour. "And where better place to start than with the entrees? While we savour those delicious morsels if you care to look up at the screen behind me, you'll see the live result of this fundraiser. I'll take this opportunity to remind you that twenty-five countries are participating in this year's appeal, and we hope to be able to raise a donation toward the DWC in excess of five hundred million dollars."

The MC paused while the audience gasped. Then, with the timing of a professional, he continued his speech. "Yes, ladies and gentlemen, that's half a billion dollars with which, I'm sure you can imagine, we would be able to change the lives of not hundreds of people, not even thousands, but millions of individuals out there who need our help."

The audience applauded. The MC raised his hands to calm them. "Following the entrees, we will be honoured with our first speaker of the evening. He's come all the way from Australia just to be here tonight. So please do give a warm British welcome to Mr Augustus Derby, who is also here with his very beautiful wife. For those who aren't aware, Mr Derby is responsible for bringing us all together here tonight. If you'd like to catch a glimpse of him, he's the one on the top table. Can't see him? Okay, here's a clue, he's the one with the tan."

The crowd laughed again, but the MC stopped them short. "We'll then break for the main course. I shall not spoil the surprise, but I hope you brought your doggy bags because we have managed to get twice-awarded Michelin star chef Patrick Du Priz to come to our little gathering and cook us up some of his finest flavourful offerings."

The crowd murmured. Most of the audience would frequently dine in some of the world's top restaurants. But they all knew that to recognise and appreciate the chef was the way to befriend him and be invited to his own restaurant at a later date.

"It is then, at exactly eight o'clock, ladies and gentlemen, that the clock will be stopped. The phone lines and internet donation service have been open now for twenty-four hours. But from that point on, no more donations will be accepted, and our guest of honour, Mr Bernard Turvey, will take over the microphone to reveal the final figure. So without further ado, let's see just how close we are to that final figure. And remember, we're looking for five hundred million dollars. Are we ready?" The MC held the microphone out to the crowd, and though many cheered, a few preferred not to make such vulgar displays of immaturity in public.

"Okay, let's count down," said the MC. "Three, two…" There was hushed silence, and then he whispered into the microphone. "One."

A huge two-hundred-inch screen above the Master of Ceremonies lit up with displays of fireworks. The lights in the room dimmed slightly, and lasers fixed to the ceiling carved their way across the room in wild, erratic circles. The display was designed to build the tension in the room, and to great effect. Then, in the centre of the screen, in massive figures above him, the number three hundred and eighty-four million appeared in bold red letters.

"So, there we go, ladies and gentlemen," continued the MC. The lights were slowly brought back up. The lasers were faded to off. "There we go. Just shy of eighty percent. We have an hour still left to run. So call your wealthy uncles, phone your friends, sell your kidneys, do whatever it takes. Let's make this year count. Let's hit that half a billion dollar target. Thank you for your time, ladies and gentlemen, please do enjoy your entrees. I shall return shortly to introduce the first of our guests. But, for now, bon appetit, everybody."

CHAPTER TWENTY-FIVE

"Okay, everyone, this is it," said Jackson to the room. "You all know the situation. Those of you looking for the bomb, carry on looking. Time is running out. Those of you not involved in the live event, keep going. Shout out anything you find, no matter how insignificant. And those of you researching the audience, keep your eyes peeled. Tenant, how many cameras do we have on the audience?"

"Dozens, sir. I've got the live feed of all the major news channels and broadcasters."

"Good, get them up on the screens. People, we need to be watching the audience. We have men at every door. If you see anything suspicious, call it out. We'll have someone take them out of the room. There's a strong chance that Crowe has someone there to make sure Bernard goes through with it. We cannot let that happen," said Jackson. "You can all see the table plan on the wall behind me. If you see someone acting suspect, call it out, gender, age, description, table number. We need to keep it as low key as possible."

Jackson approached Reg as soon as he saw the team get their

heads down. The noise in the room returned to its low hum of discussion and frantic clicking of keyboards.

"Tenant, what's the news with Dubai?"

"Harvey won't read my messages. I believe he's on the attack," replied Reg.

"You believe? We need confirmation. At no point here can we let any of this roll without our understanding."

"Affirmative, sir. I've sent him two messages. If he won't read them, I have no way of contacting him."

Jackson huffed loudly through his nose. "You know him. What's he likely to do?"

"He's a good guy, sir, despite what you've heard or read."

"You think he can stop this?"

"I think he'll rescue Melody. In fact, I have no doubt about that." Reg paused. "I can't comment on Mrs Turvey and the girl."

"You think he'd leave them there?" asked Jackson.

"I think he'll read the situation and do whatever he can with Melody as his priority."

"Mills is not our priority. She knew the dangers."

"With all due respect, sir, Harvey is not an operative. He's just a capable man looking out for his girl."

"How much does Stone know?" asked Jackson.

"He knew where to find Melody, and he knows she's in trouble," replied Reg. "What he's found out since is unknown."

"So he doesn't know about the bomb?"

"I don't know. Maybe?" Reg shrugged.

"But he knows about the demands and the repercussions?"

"Your guess is as good as mine."

"Tell me he knows that the local government need to stay out of the picture."

"I may have missed that out during my covert briefing with him on the underground, sir."

Jackson shook his head in disbelief. "Does Mills know Stone is there?"

"Bit of a risk, sir," said Reg. "It might alter her mental state. She might act before Harvey is ready, change his plan."

"Plan, Tenant?" said Jackson hopefully. "He has a plan?"

"Oh, believe me, sir; Harvey will have a plan A, B and C. Why do you think nobody ever caught him?" Reg smiled at his boss. "He's the best at what he does, sir."

CHAPTER TWENTY-SIX

Turvey stood from his seat. He winced at the sudden arrival of four large spotlights that illuminated him and followed him to the centre stage. He felt the weight of the handgun he'd pulled from the underside of the top table and stashed in his inside pocket. It felt heavy, heavier than any gun he'd carried before. It wasn't until he laid eyes on the first camera that his public speaking experience kicked in, and he straightened, suddenly aware of his posture.

He stepped up to the lectern, and the room slowly fell silent in anticipation of his speech. He heard the individual claps gradually stop, and could place the last clapping person beyond the bright lights. There was no escape now.

Turvey took a deep breath.

"When DWC was formed, I wasn't even born," he began. "In that first year, I think I'm right in saying that the equivalent value of the donation was a mere five thousand dollars, which, in those times, was a grand sum of money. But resources were low and medical research was technologically limited compared to the wonders we can achieve in today's world. That's evolution, some say, it's a natural progression. But I beg to differ. Let's consider the natural progression of the human race. Learning to walk, for instance, took us millions of years. Learning to communicate, again, took us millions of years. The difference between five thousand dollars and five hundred million dollars in only forty-five years cannot be disregarded as a natural progression."

The audience murmured, and Turvey, a practised public speaker, allowed them the chance. He knew it would add to the impact of what he was about to say.

"Forty-five years ago, one percent of the world's population was richer than the rest of the world. And guess what? That hasn't changed. We're not all wealthier. The population has grown exponentially in forty-five years, but that ninety-nine percent of the remaining wealth has just been diluted."

The audience was intrigued by the direction of his speech. Turvey spoke well. He was clear and had the nuances of a leader who guided people's imaginations.

"So if it's not a natural progression that can spark such a rise in generosity, then what is it? Do you know what I think, ladies and gentlemen in this room, and all the incredible people out there that have donated tonight to help save these poor people from a life of misery and pain?" He paused once more.

"I think it's desire."

Three hundred people sat at the tables in the room, and another hundred people stood around the edge as security, cameramen, media reporters and events crew. Not one person made a sound.

"Forget about natural progression, I want you to visualise something new. Desire. Visualise a job you once wanted. It was a job you had wanted for a long time, a great step in your long career, whatever that may be. How many other people went for that job? Ten? Twenty? Fifty? Heck, with today's internet recruitment channels, some companies see thousands of people applying for a single job. And the company gets to choose. They get to select the best of the best. But the reality is that thousands of people desire that job. And the result? The company ends up with the best person possible for that company. If they do their job right, that person will make positive changes. That person might mean the difference between a good year and a great year. That person might mean that others that were not invested in their jobs suddenly grew to become invested because that one person led them effectively. And what happens? The company lifts up a notch. It might be a small amount, it might be a great lift, but the company makes progress."

Turvey stared out at the crowd beyond the lights, not focusing on individuals, but scanning the heads in the room.

"Progress," he said. "One word. Sure, you might think the company makes progress from all those positive changes. But ladies and gentlemen, progress is not the reason. Can you see? It is the desire. It was the desire of all those thousands of other people that brought the best of the best, the cream of the cream, to the interview room. It was the desire of the organisation to progress. The organisation desired to hire the best of the best. And ladies and gentlemen, if you haven't seen the analogy, it is the desire of mankind, right here, right now, to help millions of people around the world. It is the desire of every single person who donated, no matter how big or small the donation, to make sure that those who need help get the help. Desire, ladies and gentlemen. If you want something badly enough, *you will make it happen*."

The audience burst into applause. Chairs scraped back as they stood to clap, and Mr Turvey looked down unsmiling at the praise. He had completed his work. All that remained was for him to flick the switch and display the final amount on the massive screen above.

"Before I hit this switch, ladies and gentlemen," he continued. "Before we see the final figure, I'd like to say just this. It won't be me standing here next year. I won't have the pleasure of seeing the delight in all of your smiling faces or enjoy the company of so many generous people. But I hope this charity continues. I hope that at each future gala dinner, year by year, the line from five thousand dollars to five hundred million dollars becomes even more vertical. I hope that one day, that number will be a billion dollars. And the way we do that is by raising the desire. The more people we have that want to help, the closer we'll get to our target. But you know what? More than anything, I hope in the not too distant future, maybe next year, maybe the year after, that we don't raise a penny."

Bernard said the last sentence with a cruel snarl and allowed time for the comment to be absorbed by his captive audience.

"I truly hope that in less than five years' time, this room is empty, or hosting a dance or a wedding or some other event than this one. I don't want the ninety-nine percent of the world's population having to put their hands in their pockets to help the sick. I don't even want the richest one percent of the population to pay out. Because one day, ladies and gentlemen, I believe we will break this illness, and wipe it from our planet. Every penny we've raised tonight is one step closer to that goal."

Once again, the room exploded in applause. Bernard pulled the handkerchief from his top pocket and wiped his brow. He knew his time was coming. He'd bought as much time as he could have hoped for. But his ear-piece had not burst into life to inform him that Crowe had been taken down as he had hoped. That meant that Angie and Anya were still prisoners, and all that remained was to save his family's lives.

"And now we come to the part we have all been waiting for," said Bernard. "In a moment, I shall hit stop on the clock, and the donations will cease to be accepted. The final figure will be shown on the screen above me, and we'll have a fairly accurate measurement of just how much the population of the world desire to help those that so desperately need our help."

Bernard moved his hand to the switch and noticed for the first time how unsteady his hands were. Fear gripped him. He knew with each passing second that he was one step closer to death. He glanced at Gordon at the edge of the room and was met with a saddened expression and a gentle shake of the head.

Gordon's hand raised to his ear, and suddenly, Bernard's own ear-piece crackled into life. "Just stall, sir. Take as long as you need."

Bernard regained his composure. He wiped his brow once more, and then addressed the audience who sat forward attentively.

"Shall we have a countdown?" he said. The number ten appeared in bold, colourful figures on the screen. The audience began to count down.

"Ten."

"Nine."

More people joined in the countdown, and the room felt like an Olympic stadium.

"Eight."

"Seven."

The lasers danced around the walls. Spotlights flashed from person to person, lighting up a member of the audience before moving onto the next person.

"Six."

"Five."

"The screen began to display its fireworks, as the bright red and blue numbers increased in size.

"Four."

"Three."

Bernard held onto the lectern as he looked up hopefully. He willed the money to be there. He desired it so much. If his last act could be something as significant as a half-a-billion-dollar donation to help the cause, he would at least be remembered for the occasion.

"Two."

"One."

The screen went dark. The audience hushed. The spotlights went out and the lasers died.

Then the smiling face of a man in his fifties appeared on the screen.

"Hello, London."

CHAPTER TWENTY-SEVEN

"How?" shouted Jackson at Reg, who sat with his jaw hanging open.

"I, I don't know, sir," stammered Reg. "I didn't see that coming."

"I thought you said you had control over the internet line?"

"Yes, I'm in total control of what's being sent out. But I can't see anything coming in, certainly not video traffic," said Reg.

"So how come we, and a few million other people, are staring at Caesar Crowe's face?"

"He has to be using another line. There must be-"

"Find it," snapped Jackson. "And stop it." He turned to another tech operative a few desks along from Reg. "Bailey, get the volume up on that screen."

A few seconds later, the cold voice of Caesar Crowe had filtered through into the heads of every single person in the room as they watched him captivate and bemuse the guests of the forty-fifth DWC Annual Gala Dinner.

"I realise that I am not a listed speaker at the event tonight, and I feel I should add that I did not donate this year or the year before. Perhaps that's one of the reasons I wasn't invited?"

He smiled at the camera, and the audience felt the chill of his tone.

"Alas," continued Crowe, "it is not for me to decide the audience of such a gratifying affair. I can only imagine the audience with you tonight are all very wealthy, very naïve, but very well connected. It's not what you know, it's who you know, right?"

The audience murmured and looked confusedly between Turvey on stage and the Master of Ceremonies who stood to the side.

"Speaking of knowing people," said Crowe, "the reason I have decided to hijack the final speech of tonight's charitable soirée is to allow you all the opportunity to get to know Mr Turvey. I listened with glee at his speech, and I must say, Bernie, you know how to get the crowd going, don't you?"

Bernard looked aghast. His eyes flicked from the crowds behind the glaring lights and back to the screen.

"You see," continued Crowe, "Mr Turvey here may have an exterior worthy of a place beside the Lord himself behind the pearly gates of heaven for his saint-like emotions, and heartfelt *desires*. But he does, in fact, have a few secrets of his own, and tonight, ladies and gentlemen, as a finalé, we shall reveal those secrets. So you can make your own minds up about Saint Turvey and his spot in heaven."

Crowe was as much an experienced public speaker as Bernard and held his tongue for a moment for the crowds to exchange confused chatter.

"Did you know, good people of the DWC, that your guest speaker tonight, the man that chairs the entire DWC operation..." Crowe put his hand up to his mouth as if revealing a secret. "Did you know he's actually a senior member of MI6? Now you do. It's true, you know. How can any of God's angels lie? Look at him. He cannot deny it. Can you, Bernie?"

Bernard straightened. His career was top secret, but there was nothing he could do to prevent the exposure now. Instead, he stared resolutely at Crowe.

"Some of you may have had ideas about Mr Turvey's career in law enforcement. Some of you may have no idea. But the best secrets are the ones that come with a surprise, don't you think? Some of you may even wonder how a man such as Bernie here actually makes it into MI6, and I would wonder too, if I didn't know the truth. You see, ladies and gentlemen, the man who stands before you tonight is a very, very bad man. But tonight, we shall give him the opportunity to resurrect his soul. I'm not talking about the five hundred and fifteen million dollars that have been raised tonight. Yes, five hundred and fifteen million dollars, people. You beat your target by fifteen million dollars.

"But I digress. I'm not talking about Bernie saving his soul by being an empty voice and flicking a switch to create a snowball effect whereby thousands of volunteers work for nothing in the most God-awful places on the planet to save a bunch of ungrateful, lazy and unintelligent people from a life of suffering, as their sins decreed. No. I'm talking about the man behind the facade. I'm talking about the rotten, stinking soul of Bernard Turvey and his so-called *desires*.

"You see, a long time ago, before the internet, and seemingly when the world was a larger place, it was impossible to reach out to people across a fibre optic network to ask for help. It was impossible to make a call on your mobile phone to raise an alarm. However, it was possible for people like Bernard Turvey to torture and kill innocent people and go unnoticed."

Crowe allowed a few seconds for the crowd to become inquisitive. Turvey stood straight on the stage, but the glares and horrified stares began to find his flesh. He began to sink. He knew what was coming next.

"You see, Bernard Turvey was once a mere foot soldier, an

apprentice among the best. Britain's finest. He had ambition. He had desires, ladies and gentlemen. He'd smelled the glory and seen people rise quickly in the ranks; he wanted that for himself. Myself, I was a criminal. I'm not ashamed to say it, not because it's in my past, but because, well, to be frank, the opinions of those of you listening matter to me not. I stole, not from the poor, no, I was raised better than that, but I carved earnings from institutions. I shaved pennies from organisations, unnoticed. I stole from that one percent of people your fabled guest speaker spoke of earlier, not the ninety-nine percent of the population who had to share the petty remains of the global wealth.

"I did well, but over time, I admit, greed took hold of me. Eventually, I made a mistake. It was catastrophic. One might say my desires outgrew my capabilities. One day, I woke up staring at the painful end of Mr Turvey's gun. Not at first, but as my eyes adjusted to the morning light and my brain began to understand that it was all over, I began to accept it. I'd been caught. I was ready to stand, dress and be taken away. And had it been another member of Britain's finest and not a power-hungry, ladder-climber such as Bernie, that is exactly how the next few moments would have played out. I had no gun in my hand. I made no attempt to get away, and neither did my wife. It was as she woke, and rolled over to kiss her husband on the cheek, that she saw the gun. Frightened, as you can imagine, she jumped up and began to scramble out of bed."

Crowe's voice broke, slightly, a play on the memory aimed to bring the audience to his side.

"That was when old twitchy fingers Turvey here shot her dead."

The crowd gasped.

"Not once, ladies and gentlemen, not twice, but three times. Once in the back of the head and two more to finish her off while she lay on the floor. I thank God that she was dead before the second and third bullets touched her."

Crowe gave a sombre, downcast look, and then continued his story.

"Then I made a run for it. This was no longer a game of cops and robbers. I was no longer going to say that it was fair cop guv'nor, and allow myself to be handcuffed. This man was out for blood. I made it as far as the bedroom door when the first bullet hit me in the shoulder. I still have the scar. But as I snatched open the bedroom door and let it crash into the wall beside me, I looked down for a brief moment. I saw the face of an angel staring back at me. My child."

Crowe silenced, and the room silenced with him.

"Then her face just seemed to cave in, as the bullets tore her apart in front of my eyes."

The audience noise shot up and Bernard clasped his eyes closed, wishing this nightmare would end.

"I ran, of course," said Crowe. "I ran for all I had, and by some misguided fortune, Bernard Turvey here wasn't arresting me as part of a crack squad of MI5 agents. He was, in fact, operating alone. He was seeking the glory he so very much desired. So I made my escape. The tragic deaths of my family were covered over, and the blame put on some crazed burglar who was never found. Ladies and gentlemen, does that sound like the type of man who would sit beside God himself and command the angels?"

People began to stand to leave the room. But Crowe raised the volume of his speech and caught the attention of them all.

"And then there's poor Mrs Turvey. Oh yes, the story continues. You see, as shambolic as my previous story was, there's more. Oh yes. He wasn't content with his elevated position in the prestigious MI6. He wasn't content with chairing one of the world's largest charities."

Crowe's voice dropped to a caring whisper.

"He wasn't content either with being lucky enough to have the support and devotion of the very beautiful Angela Turvey, and their even more beautiful daughter, Anya Turvey. No, he had to get his thrills elsewhere. He had to fulfil his desires, you see?" Crowe paused and looked around the room. "How do I know all this? How do I know that Mr Turvey's family are so worthy of gratitude and respect? How do I know they're so beautiful?"

Crowe smiled.

"They're right here with me."

CHAPTER TWENTY-EIGHT

Crowe moved away from the camera and allowed the global audience a view of the Turvey's Dubai holiday home. To the left was Angie Turvey, stripped naked and tied to what looked like the corpse of another woman, who was tied to fixings in the wall. In the centre of the screen sat Anya Turvey. Her wrists and ankles were bound with duct tape, and to the right of the screen was another woman dressed in black. She had also been bound and was unable to move.

The three women stared at the screen, and the horrified audience gasped collectively. An elderly woman dressed in a flowery dress and her finest pearls fainted and slipped from her chair. Two men either side rushed to tend her.

"Stop," shouted Turvey. He held onto the lectern as if his life depended on it. "Enough is enough. I'll do it."

"You'll wait and do exactly what you're told," replied Crowe, coming back into the camera's view. "These people deserve to hear the rest of my story. These people deserve to know the truth about the monster behind the shiny, idyllic illusion you cast. You see, good people of the DWC, Mr Turvey has a whole range of tastes. I'm in his home now and I can tell you, it is exquisitely designed and finished with the finest materials money can buy. The table that this laptop rests on is worth more than ten thousand dollars, and that's just the table. If you sold the art in this house, you could feed a village of starving children in Asia for a month. So, when Bernie here tells us all about his so-called heroic attempts at destroying the terrible affliction for what DWC stands to quell, ask yourself this: how much did he actually donate tonight?"

The crowd had fallen silent again. Bernard Turvey leaned against the lectern, unable to face the screen and look into the eyes of the man that had destroyed his family and his reputation. It no longer mattered that the charity had smashed the target. It was all over.

"Nothing," spat Crowe. "Zero. That's how much he donated to the cause he so strongly believes in. Yet he pleaded with you all to make sure you gave whatever you could afford, didn't he? Desire, ladies and gentlemen. Let's talk about Bernie's desires and his tastes, as I believe that for this next part of my speech, they are most appropriate."

Crowe's face was moved out of focus, and a printed photo of Bernard Turvey with two young and expensive-looking prostitutes was placed in front of the camera.

"That's not Angie Turvey, I can assure you all. Angie here has far more class than that. No, these girls are nothing but high-class prostitutes sought from a high-class escort agency. It may seem as if they are simply enjoying dinner with a well-dressed, tanned businessman. But on that particular night, the fun didn't stop there."

The photo was replaced with another. The second image showed Bernard Turvey in bed with the two girls. The room was disgusted. A man at the front shouted an insult at Bernard and made to leave with his wife. But Crowe stopped him with a loud and old command. "*Sit down.*"

The man looked up at the screen.

"Yes, you, the one with no hair and the suit that looks like your grandfather bought it before the war, *sit down*."

The man reddened and sat, looking indignant and wholly embarrassed.

"Would you like to see more?" Crowe addressed the entire room again. He then replaced the image with one of Bernard Turvey tied to the same bed, but in a state of submission and humiliation. He was clearly aroused as the two leather-clad girls wore various arrangements of strap-on sex toys.

"Shocking, isn't it?" said Crowe. "This is the man you all came to see. The man you all came to hear talk about how wonderful this charity is. Look at him squirm on the stage in front of you all."

Many of the women in the audience had looked away from the screen, horrified at what they had seen.

"We all know these things happen. We all know that there are people out there who enjoy a fruitful sex life. But do you all honestly think that Mrs Turvey here deserves to be so mistreated?" Crowe moved to one side to allow the audience a view of the woman who stood behind him, tied to the corpse of her neighbour. "However," he continued, "I regret to inform you all that our dear friend, Bernie, is even sicker than you might quite imagine."

Crowe looked sorrowfully at the camera as if the news he was about to deliver was against his own will. "Ladies and gentlemen, I give you Bernard Turvey in all his glory."

Once more, Crowe's face disappeared from view as the final photo crept into the frame.

CHAPTER TWENTY-NINE

"Oh my God," said Jackson. "How do we stop this?"

"I can't stop the video traffic going into the event. But I can stop the traffic from leaving the Turvey house where it's originating from," said Reg.

"Do it," replied Jackson.

"Once I kill it though, we'll have no way of getting back in there, and we won't have eyes on the family." Reg leaned back in his chair. "It's your call, sir. We've been trying to get a handle on what's going on in the house for two days. We now have eyes on the inside."

Jackson dropped his head into his hands and peered through his fingers in despair.

"Let's face it," continued Reg, "it can't get much worse, can it?"

Suddenly, Crowe's cold voice tore through the speakers. "I think we've all seen enough of our friend, Bernie, haven't we? I hope that you can all see that the man stood on the stage before you is not all he seems. I also feel that now is the time to let the rest of the world know exactly what's coming next."

The ambient hum of the audience dropped once more as

the outraged and disgusted people turned their attention back to the face on the screen.

"Mr Turvey, do you want to tell the rest of the world what you are going to do?" said Crowe. "Or should I?"

Bernard Turvey stood rocking on the stage. He stared unblinkingly at the floor for what seemed like an eternity before raising his head and speaking to the audience. Lowering his mouth to the microphone, he looked out at the horrified faces then took a deep breath.

"I could stand here and defend myself, defend my honour, and defend my family name. I could stand here and plead with you all for forgiveness and try to regain your trust. But the fact of the matter is..."

He paused, as if the words he spoke next would strike him down.

"Yes?" said Crowe. "Go on, Bernie."

Bernard's eyes flicked up to the screen and back to the crowd; they were wet, glistening with the high-powered spots that seemed to burn right through him.

"It's true," he said. "It's all true."

As if the audience doubted Crowe's allegations, they gasped in unison once more, Turvey's words somehow cementing the facts.

"And what are we going to do about it?" asked Crowe. "What do you have to say to all these nice people that were sucked in by your cruel and perverse desires?"

"Words cannot describe how I feel right now," said Bernard. "To the audience and the public, I am truly ashamed. I abused my position, I abused my power, and I abused my wealth for my own satisfaction."

"That's a start," said Crowe. "Who in the audience wants to see old Bernie here suffer?"

The room remained quiet for a while. Then somewhere near the back of the room, a man shouted out, "Make him pay."

Another joined in. "Yeah, make him donate all his money."

"Make him resign," shouted another.

"All good ideas," said Crowe. "But I was thinking of something a little more permanent. You know, a payment so true that even God himself couldn't undo the changes, even if he wanted to."

"Send him down," cried a woman from the front of the crowd.

"Yeah, lock him up."

"Send him where?" asked Crowe. "To prison? So you can keep paying for him with your hard-earned taxes. Is that what you really want?"

The room quietened once more.

"No, I didn't think so," said Crowe.

In the operations room, Jackson calmly addressed his team. "This is it. Be ready to-"

"I've lost my connection," said Reg. There was a sudden urgency in his usually calm voice.

"You've what?" asked Jackson.

"I can't get on. I'm being kicked out of the firewall."

"Well, can't you get back on?"

"I'm trying but-"

"But what?" cried Jackson. "You know what comes next, don't you?"

"Of course I know what comes next," snapped Reg. "But we're being attacked ourselves. He must have bots. It's a denial of service attack."

"Now is not the time to play games, Tenant."

"He's right, sir," said the girl beside Reg. "We have a dedicated line, and it's as much as I can do to fend off the attacks. They're coming from everywhere."

A woman's scream brought the focus back to the event, and all eyes returned to the live feed from the dinner.

Bernard stood in the centre of the stage with a gun in his hand. He pulled the cocking lever back and let the mechanism collect a round from the magazine. Then he placed the weapon against his temple.

CHAPTER THIRTY

The startled audience winced as Angie Turvey screamed at her husband from behind Crowe. The shrill high pitch caused the speakers to crackle, and Crowe spun in his seat.

"That's right Bernie, you get the idea," said Crowe, turning back to the screen. "Is there anything you'd like to say to Angie before you go?"

"Mummy," yelled Anya from the couch. "Mummy, I'm scared."

Angie ignored her daughter and yelled at the laptop. "Bernie, *no.*"

Bernard Turvey's face was bright red. His sunken eyes were like black holes, as the adrenaline, fear and horror of the past few days approached its climax.

"Angie," he called, his throat thick with shame, "Angie, I'm so sorry. I never meant for this."

Angie pulled at her restraints and Julie's body rocked limply with her attempts. "Don't do it, Bernie. Please, don't do it."

"I don't have a choice, baby," replied Bernard. His hand shook with the weapon, and he forced the muzzle into his head. "There's no way back from this."

Two armed policemen approached the stage, but Crowe saw them at the edge of the screen and called them off.

"Baby, no," screamed Angie. Her knees gave way, and she fell against her bindings. Julie's head bounced softly against her naked chest.

"Mummy." Floods of tears streamed from Anya's eyes as she looked at her mother's stress. Her voice trailed off to a high-pitched whine, and then loud, uncontrollable crying.

"Angie, I'm sorry," said Bernard. "I have to do this. For you." He broke and sobbed loudly. The stress of the situation had blinded him to the audience. He pulled at his hair with his free hand, and jerked his head into his chest, then with a loud, agitated groan, he straightened.

"I'm sorry, baby," said Angie. "I'm sorry I put you through hell. I'm sorry I wasn't a better wife. We can work it out. I understand. I don't care what you did, just put the gun down."

"Bernie?" said Crowe, interjecting. "You know what you need to do, don't you?"

Bernard was sobbing uncontrollably now, along with his daughter who had her face buried in the cushions of the couch, unable to move.

"Bernie, are you ignoring me?" said Crowe coldly.

"You sick son of a bitch," replied Bernard.

"Pull the trigger, Bernie."

"No, baby, no," yelled Angie. "We can move away. We can start again."

It was at that moment that Crowe pulled his own handgun from his waistband, and moved from the laptop toward Angie.

The crowd was deathly silent. Women cried and turned away. The armed police all looked for direction from a man at the edge of the room, who held one hand up to halt them and, with the other hand, held his finger to his ear, talking to his own bosses on his ear-piece.

Crowe stood behind Angie, whose face was buried behind Julie's cold and stiffening legs. He grabbed a handful of hair and pulled her head back, turning her face to the laptop.

"Look at him," he said. "I want you to watch him."

"Get your hands off her, you coward," snarled Bernard, aggression cutting through the fear.

"Bernie," wailed Angie in a long hopeless whimper. "I love you, Bernie. I always did, and I always will."

"Now, damn it," snapped Crowe. "Pull the God damned trigger."

The audience's eyes flicked back to Turvey in anticipation.

Bernard's entire arm shook involuntarily. The gun hit his head each time until he pressed it firmly into his skull again.

"Do it, Turvey," shouted Crowe. "Or I'll do it."

Bernard's arm folded firmly as if all the effort it took him to pull the trigger came from his shoulder.

Crowe slammed his handgun into the side of Angie's head, and she crumpled along with Julie's body, unconscious. He stepped across the room and grabbed the back of Anya's top with his free hand.

Melody launched herself on the couch to stop him, but Anya's legs were already in the air as he hoisted her over the back of the chair to stand beside her unconscious mother. She didn't scream. She was visibly crying, but she didn't whimper. Anya just stared at her mother's face, as if looking up at her father on the screen would somehow make it worse.

"Now, Bernie, would you care to re-think that?" said Crowe.

"Anya," said Bernard. His desperate voice shook Anya from her gaze, and she looked up at him as if guilty of some childish action. "Anya, it's me, baby. Everything's going to be okay. I promise you. Are you hurt?"

Anya stared at him on the screen with the audience behind him.

"Anya, baby, are you hurt?

She shook her head slowly then lowered it again.

"That's it, baby. I want you to look away. Close your eyes and remember the day we had on the beach. You remember that, don't you? Don't you baby? The house at the beach. Remember how we swam and all the little fishes came to us?"

The girl looked up at the screen again and nodded.

"Good, I want you to close your eyes, and think of that day. Can you do that?"

The girl's face crumpled into a loud sob, and she shook her head. "No, Daddy, I'm scared."

"It's okay. You don't need to be scared, baby. You can do this. You're a big girl now, aren't you?"

Her wide eyes glistened on the large screen above Bernard, and a woman in the audience called out to Crowe, "Take her away, you monster. She can't see this."

Crowe sensed the audience's growing impatience. "Bernard, you have precisely ten seconds to say goodbye to your daughter. Or I'll finish them both."

"Anya, baby, close your eyes. Please just close your eyes, okay? I love you baby, more than anything in the world. Please just close your eyes, and I'll be with you forever. Wherever you go, I'll be by your side, baby. Okay?"

The girl nodded at the screen.

"Okay, are you ready to close your eyes?" asked Bernard. His voice trembled as he said goodbye to his daughter.

She nodded once more.

"Okay, baby. I love you, remember that."

Anya closed her eyes.

Bernard raised the gun to his head for the last time.

"Okay, Turvey," began Crowe, "the world has seen who you really are. The evidence is irrefutable." He smiled cruelly at the camera and placed the gun behind Anya's head. "Pull the trigger, Bernie."

Bernard's face was a mess of sweat, tears and emotion. His hand quivered for all to see, so he moved the gun to his mouth and tilted his head back. The packed hall was as silent as it could be.

"*Do it*," shouted Crowe. He opened his foul mouth once more. But instead of another onslaught of bitter, cold words, a trickle of blood ran across his lower lip and dribbled onto his chin. His eyes opened wide. Then slowly, and as if it grew from deep inside him, the shiny point of a nine-inch carving knife emerged from his mouth.

CHAPTER THIRTY-ONE

Confusion spread throughout the audience, and people stood as if sitting somehow obscured the truth behind the unbelievable turn of events.

The man in black twisted the blade to the right with a crunch of gristle and bone. As the life slipped out of Caesar Crowe's body, and gravity took effect, he slipped slowly off the blade and crumpled to the floor at the newcomer's feet. The shadow stood tall over Caesar's body, emotionless, a dark silhouette against the now-moonlit curtains. He remained motionless for what seemed like an eternity, but the struggles of the woman on the couch caught his eye, and he turned the blade on her. He stepped over Caesar Crowe and slit the tape that bound the woman. The crowd sighed collectively, a deep sigh of relief. The trauma was over.

The woman pulled her wrists free, flung her arms around the stranger, and kissed him hard on the mouth. This time, chairs scraped against the floor, and the noise in the room grew from the hushed silence of the shocked but captivated audience to a deafening roar of applause and cheers. Even the media presenters who had also been enthralled by the night's events clapped.

She pulled away and took the blade from the man in black. After cutting her own ankle restraints, she began to free the little girl and her mother, who had to be calmed down as she frantically tore herself away from the corpse. The second she was free, she reached down and scooped up her daughter. She then sat on the couch with the girl on her lap and began rocking gently back and forth, smoothing the child's hair.

The stage was rushed by armed guards, who took the weapon from Bernard Turvey and held him upright as his knees gave way. They dragged the ruined man away, and the ever-professional Master of Ceremonies took to the stage in an attempt to control the riot of people trying to leave the hall.

A dark-haired man remained seated, while others fought to leave. He stared coldly at the large screen that, by now, showed the woman pulling a blanket around Mrs Turvey and the little girl and lowering herself to her knees to console the distraught pair. The man, in his late forties with a crooked nose and cleft lip, stood, straightened his bow tie, downed the remains of his drink, and then joined the queue of people at the doors.

CHAPTER THIRTY-TWO

Jackson fell back into the chair that was behind him. The room full of operatives had not cheered, had not clapped; they hadn't broken a smile. The sequence of events that had played out so dramatically in front of theirs, and a million other people's eyes, had merely altered the plan and set a new objective.

Melody's voice, controlled and calm, began to ring loud and clear through the speaker beside Reg.

"Reg, do you copy?" she asked.

Reg gave a tight smile at the girl, Jess, who sat beside him, and then pushed the push-to-talk button on the microphone. "Loud and clear, Melody, loud and clear. It's never been so good to hear your voice."

Melody waited a few seconds, and then replied, "Yeah, it was getting close there for a minute."

"Okay, you sound like you have everything under control there. But I need you to help me with something."

"Sure," said Melody. "What do I need to do?"

"Was he on a laptop? Was that where the video feed was coming from?"

"Yeah, it's right here. You need me to shut it down?"

"No," said Reg, a little sharper than he needed. "Are there any other programmes running on it?"

Melody was quiet then she said, "Not much. But wait, there's a remote session. Looks like a black box with red and blue lines of code or something."

"That's it," said Reg. "That's what we need to stop."

"I just closed the black box," said Melody. "Did that work?"

Reg glanced up at his screen then across at Jess, who nodded with a smile and mouthed the words. "We're back online."

"You did it," said Reg. "Good work. You may want to shut the laptop down; you still have a pretty large audience."

Melody turned the camera off and was about to shut the laptop down when Reg hit the push-to-talk button again. "Melody, are you still there?"

"Of course, you're in my ear," she replied.

"We may have a bit of a problem," said Reg.

The sentence roused Jackson from his daze. He sat up and stared across at Reg who was looking worriedly at Jess.

"Are you sure no other programmes were running?" asked Reg.

"Of course I'm sure," said Melody.

"Well, don't make yourselves too comfy there," continued Reg. "I think you just set the timer on the bomb."

CHAPTER THIRTY-THREE

"How do you know?" asked Melody. "How long do we have?"

Harvey sensed the sudden urgency in Melody's voice. "What's wrong?"

Melody looked across the room to where Harvey had begun to drag Crowe's body beside Omar's. "Reg thinks we just triggered the timer on the bomb."

"There's a timer?" he asked.

"Here's what I see," began Reg. "It looks like there was a constant exchange of traffic between the laptop and another device. It's not uncommon. They're called keep-alives. They're normally set to ping one another at set intervals to make sure the other is still alive. However, if for some reason, one of the devices fail, the one that's still alive can be programmed to carry out a certain function, such as search for the device, shutdown, or-"

"Detonate?" said Melody.

Harvey heard only Melody's side of the conversation and leaned on the back of the couch with his arms folded. "Can you get Reg up on the screen?" he asked.

Melody fired the laptop back up, and Reg continued to talk.

"It looks like when we shut the program down, the keep alive was met with a final command. One word. Begins with D."

"Hey Reg, are you able to get on the laptop so we can all talk?" said Melody.

"Yeah sure, I'm just getting on now," he replied.

A few moments later, Reg's face appeared on the screen. Melody saw that he was sat in his usual position with his feet up under the desk, a can of soft drink in front of him and his keyboard on his lap.

"Good evening, Dubai," said Reg.

"Reg how do we stop this?" asked Melody.

"We've no way of knowing where it is," said Reg. "It could be in the house. It could be anywhere."

"What about his phone?" said Harvey. "If we gave you his phone, could you trace where it's been?"

Reg thought on it. "I can only see where it was when it made calls. The interaction would be logged. So as long as he made a call somewhere close."

Harvey began to rifle through Crowe's pockets and retrieved his phone.

"It's here. What do you need us to do, Reg?" said Harvey.

"Pull the SIM out. What's the number?"

Harvey read the printed number on the SIM card out loud and waited for Reg's confirmation.

"Okay, here we go," said Reg. "It's a burner, but it's loaded with data. And hey, look." Reg caught the attention of Jess beside him, and the two tech gurus smiled and high-fived.

"Are you guys celebrating?" asked Melody.

"Sorry, Melody," said Reg. "But Jess here has been working on a program that dissects the historical data saved in the maps function inside the search engine."

"That's awesome. But how does that help us?" asked Harvey.

"Well, if I just share my screen with you both." Reg clicked his mouse a few times, and the camera view of London was replaced with a live view of Reg's screen. It displayed a map of Dubai. "Do you see all these little dots here that form a long red line?" asked Reg.

"Yeah, we see them," said Melody.

"Okay, so in GPS talk, they're called-"

"Way-points," finished Melody. "That's Crowe's movements. He doesn't know his way around Dubai, so he used the maps app on his phone."

"All the data we need is here," said Reg.

"So where's the bomb?" asked Harvey. "It looks like he's been all over the city."

"It looks like he has, but in most cases, he was just passing through," said Reg.

"Where has he spent the most time?" asked Melody.

"Hi, Melody, Jess here," began Jess. "I hope you don't mind me jumping in on this?"

"Hi Jess, you do what you need to do. Just find us that bomb."

"Well, I can't find you the bomb itself, but I can show you this. You see this dot here?" Jess circled the dot on the map that represented the house on the Palm Jumeirah.

"Yeah, sure," said Melody.

"Now watch. If you click on the way-point, you can see that he was there for forty-eight hours."

"That makes sense," said Melody.

"Okay, so now let's go all the way over here." Jess dragged the mouse across the screen, away from the blue that represented the ocean, past the mass of buildings that represented the city, and into the flat yellow space that represented the desert. A thin trail of way-points led from the Turvey house and meandered into the desert, stopping at an area on the map that looked to be the very edge of civilisation. The buildings came to a halt with wild desert behind them. The dot was in the centre of a large walled villa, on a street with other large walled villas.

"I know that place," said Melody.

"What?" said Reg. "How?"

"Remember the safe house I had to go to before I came here?" asked Melody. "I had to meet a guy called Bob."

"Yes, but that was an operative," said Reg. "Why would he-"

"Well," said Melody, "either Crowe wasn't who we thought he was, or Bob isn't who he says he is."

"We do have one more problem," said Jess.

"Go ahead, Jess," said Harvey.

"It looks like when you woke up Crowe's phone, it had a message waiting to send."

"Okay, so what?" said Harvey.

"Well now it's sent," replied Jess, matter-of-factly.

"So what did it say?" asked Melody.

"It's a distress call," said Jess, "to the Dubai police."

CHAPTER THIRTY-FOUR

Jackson slipped out of the operations room and took the fire escape stairs to the next floor. He found the old man in his office staring out the window with his chin resting on his joined fingers.

"Did you see it?" asked Jackson.

"I doubt anyone with a TV or a laptop in the UK missed it, Jackson," replied the old man. "It'll probably get an award for the highest rankings in history. Hostages, a live suicide attempt and a murder, that's about as good as it gets."

"It was all part of your plan, wasn't it?"

"You catch on quick, Jackson."

"What about the bomb?"

"Not part of the plan," replied the old man.

"It could destroy us."

"It probably will destroy us. So why aren't you downstairs finding it?"

"I can't see your angle on this. It's all just a game to you, isn't it?"

The old man span in his seat slowly to face Jackson. "If this is a game, Jackson, then I'm happy to say that Turvey just lost,

Crowe is out, and Stone is about to die. Not a bad result if I do say so myself."

"If that bomb goes off, sir, then we're all out," said Jackson. "Dubai will think it was us, all ties will be severed, and nearly a million Brits will be trapped in a suddenly very hostile place." Jackson stepped forward and placed his hands flat on the old man's desk. "And that's just the best-case scenario. Do you understand?"

"Jackson, firstly get your hands off my desk. Secondly, if the bomb detonates, do you think it will be me in the firing line?"

"Firing line? What are you talking about? We're talking about people's lives here."

"Answer the question, Jackson." The old man eyed him with the satisfaction of his own cunning.

"No. I doubt it," replied Jackson.

"Who do you think it will be?"

"Stone, I guess, and Mills. It'll be them who won't be coming home."

"True, but I doubt the PM will be overly excited about a relationship with the safest place in the Middle East being destroyed over an emotional ploy to rescue a man's wife and daughter without his consent. And who was it that made that decision, Jackson? Who organised the mission to rescue the Turveys? It wasn't me."

Jackson shook his head in disbelief.

"So will he come after me?" asked the old man rhetorically. "I don't think so."

"You're framing me?" said Jackson. "After all this, it's me who's going to carry this?"

"Framing is such a negative word, Jackson," said the old man. "I prefer to call it schooling."

"Are you insane? This is international relationships we're

talking about here. We're not in the playground arguing over who broke a window."

"I know precisely what we're talking about, and it is what you make it. If you want to make it international, here." The old man slid the desk phone across the shiny, wooden surface. "Use this, call the PM. I have his number if you want it. But if you want to make it in this world, Jackson, stop being so emotional, get yourself downstairs and lead." The old man sat back in his chair. "Oh, and as for best-case scenario, I'll tell you exactly what you should be hoping for. Stone finds the bomb before it detonates. The police find Stone and nail him for murder. The Dubai government remain totally unaware of the bomb and any involvement with British MI6."

Jackson stared disbelievingly at the old man. He couldn't believe that after all he had done to climb the ladder, the risks he had taken with his life, the arses he had kissed, and the crap he had to put up with, he was given a choice, and neither option was good. He could either get Stone and Mills out, potentially devastate the ties between the UAE and the UK and destroy his career, or he could play the game.

"You know what to do, Jackson," said the old man. "Do it well, and you might even find yourself in Turvey's office. The seat is still warm, I hear."

CHAPTER THIRTY-FIVE

"We need to go," said Melody. "Now."

"Hold on," said Reg over the webcam. "Take the laptop with you. It will tie the murder directly to the UK."

Harvey dug through Crowe's pockets again and found the car keys he'd heard rattling earlier. He glanced across at Melody and, with an unspoken gesture, told her they were taking the car. He walked calmly toward the garage.

"Get me on the comms, Reg," said Melody as she slammed the lid of the laptop and followed Harvey out of the room.

Melody stopped and caught Angie's attention. "Hey, are you coming?"

Angie glanced up with tired eyes and pulled the blanket around her. She shook her head. "No. No, I think we'll stay."

"Are you going to be okay?" asked Melody. "The police are-"

"On their way," finished Angie. "Yes, I know."

"What are you going to tell them?"

Angie cast her eyes to the floor, as memories of the previous few days ran through her mind. "We came into the house and were taken hostage," she replied. "It's the truth."

"What about these guys?" asked Melody, gesturing at the two dead men.

"We were saved." Angie looked up at Melody once more. "It's Melody, right?"

Melody nodded softly.

"Go, Melody, get away from this place. You don't know what they'll do if they catch you. I'll handle it. I always do."

Melody began to say something but stopped herself. Instead, she turned and followed Harvey out the door.

"Melody," called Angie.

Melody stopped once more and turned to face the woman, who looked down at her sleeping daughter in her arms.

"Thank you," said Angie. "For everything."

Melody smiled, then turned and left the room.

Harvey stepped into the garage and found a little blue Porsche beside a BMW SUV. The key fob had a Porsche symbol on, so he hit the unlock button and the door locks popped open. Melody climbed into the passenger seat beside Harvey, as he hit the button for the garage door to open.

The dark night was giving way to a fresh new day, and traces of reds and oranges began to show between the high-rise buildings on the mainland. Harvey drove steadily, not wanting to catch anybody's attention. The road off the Palm Jumeirah was already growing busy. Residents of the apartment blocks that lined the trunk of the Palm were beginning their morning commute.

The little Porsche seemed to be at home among the expensive SUVs and sports cars on the road. Harvey soon found that driving slowly and carefully was getting him nowhere. So as soon they reached the mainland, he pulled out into the fast lane and joined the speeding motorists.

Melody held the tiny button on her ear-piece for a few seconds until she heard the beeps indicating that the channel was closed. Communication with Reg would now require her to push the little button, but she wanted to talk to Harvey.

"What are you doing?" asked Melody.

"Blending in," replied Harvey. "Are you going to tell me where we're going?"

"I didn't mean the driving, Harvey," snapped Melody. "I meant what are you doing here?"

Harvey didn't reply.

"Don't play the silent card with me, Harvey. How did you find out where I was?"

"Intuition," said Harvey with a smile.

"You followed me?" she asked. "Is that it? Why? Did you think I couldn't handle it anymore?"

Harvey didn't reply.

"You told me to go, remember? I could have just left it for someone else."

"It's what you wanted," said Harvey. "I was holding you back."

"That's *my* choice," Melody yelled. "It's not your choice to make." She lowered her voice and spoke softly. "You gave me an ultimatum. How do you think that makes me feel?"

"How do you think you'd have felt if you hadn't come and helped?" said Harvey. "Do you honestly think that we'd still be in France playing happy families? You'd have spent the past two days regretting it and probably ended up resenting me. You needed a kick start, so-"

"So you kicked me?" finished Melody.

"Yeah, and I'd do the same again if I had the choice."

"I'm not the type of girl that appreciates being kicked, Harvey. You can't just tell me to go and then show up three thousand miles away. It doesn't work like that."

Harvey dropped the car into third gear, popped the clutch, and carved across the four-lane highway onto the shoulder. Cars honked their horns and swerved to miss them, but Harvey was unmovable.

He slammed on the brakes and the little sports car slid to a stop.

"I don't know what I'm doing, Melody," he began. His voice was raised, but he didn't shout. Harvey never shouted. "I've never done this, I've never felt like this, and I've never wanted someone so badly in all my life." He sat back in his seat and faced the front. "If I did it wrong, then so what, I did it wrong. But at least I did something. And if there's a next time, you know what? I'll probably get it wrong again, but I'll still try."

Melody leaned across the small centre console and put her hand on his cheek. Then she kissed him. Harvey returned the kiss and then pulled her away. He just stared at her.

"You didn't do too badly," said Melody. "Now let's go and stop this bomb."

CHAPTER THIRTY-SIX

"There you are. I thought we'd lost you there for a while," said Reg when Melody opened up the channel on her ear-piece again. Jess saw the smile on his face when Melody's voice came through the speaker.

"Technical hitch, Reg," said Melody. "We're back, so tell us where to go." Her voice was tinny and weak over the satellite comms, but she was recognisable.

"Okay, so we've got two choices," said Reg. "The villa in the desert is a twenty-mile drive. Jess pulled up the data, and it looks like Crowe spent a few days there before the Turvey house."

"Have you run a background check on the Bob guy?" asked Melody. "Is he in on this? Is he dirty?"

"I'm waiting for Jackson to get back. He got the contact from higher up. There's a chain of command here, you know?"

"You mean there's more red tape?" asked Melody.

"Oodles of it," replied Reg.

"You said we had two choices. Where else did Crowe go?" asked Melody.

"Well, he's certainly been sightseeing," replied Reg.

"So it could be anywhere?" said Melody.

"My money is on Dubai Mall," said Reg. "It's a huge tourist attraction."

"That's a big mall," replied Melody. "Are we looking for a needle here?"

"Yeah, it's a small needle in a very large haystack. But it's the safest bet."

"How do we know he wasn't shopping or meeting someone?"

"Well, unless he was shopping for six hours."

"Six hours?" said Melody. "What was he doing there for six hours?"

"Planting a bomb probably," said Reg. "But hey, I've been thinking."

Jess slapped his arm suddenly and gave him a stern look.

"Okay, Jess and I have been think-"

"Jess and you?" said Melody, grinning over at Harvey who smirked back. "Have you found your match, Reggie?"

Reg blushed, and Jess turned back to her screen, too embarrassed to face Reg.

"Anyway," Reg continued, "we were thinking that wherever he placed the device would need a fairly strong signal for the keep-alives. He wouldn't risk it detonating accidentally while he was still in the country. He's a British citizen. He'd be locked in, just as you would be and all the other Brits."

"So that rules out the basement parking, and probably the lower floors as well," said Melody.

"Agreed. But it would also need to be small enough to carry in a pack or something. Security is tight. You can't just drive in with a delivery, they're booked in advance. We did the research."

"Okay, so it's backpack size?" asked Melody.

"Has to be," said Reg. "But also, the mall is spotless. It's hit by an army of cleaners every night. They'd find a backpack lying around easily."

"So what is it? In a shop?"

"We don't know. But we're looking for somewhere on the upper floors, somewhere accessible by the public, and somewhere a small backpack could be hidden."

"Not much to go on, Reg."

"Isn't that always the case?" he replied.

"Any idea when this thing is supposed to go off?" asked Melody.

"No clue. But we do know that the mall opens to the public at ten in the morning. So you have four hours to get yourselves in there."

"I just found something," said Jess.

Reg span back to face her.

"Shoot, Jess. What did you find?"

"Something is happening in the mall this morning. It's on the website."

"Like what?" asked Melody. "What's the connection?"

"Someone important is visiting," said Jess, reading off the website. "Someone called Sheikha Alia bin something."

"Sheikha what?" replied Melody. "You *do* know what a Sheikha is, right?"

Jess looked at Reg, who looked equally as confused. Reg typed the name into a search browser.

"Oh God," he said.

"What?" asked Jess? "Who is it?"

"It's one of the Sheik's daughters."

CHAPTER THIRTY-SEVEN

Harvey and Melody ditched the Porsche on the seventh floor of the mall car park and walked swiftly but calmly to the entrance. The glass doors slid back silently, and the pair were hit with sandalwood-perfumed air conditioning in the lobby. Another set of glass doors opened, and they stepped into the huge expanse of the mall. The stores that ran left and right were all closed. A huge atrium filled the centre of the space.

Melody spoke quietly to Reg. "Hey, this place is huge. Have we got any idea at all where to look?"

Reg's tinny voice came back, calm as ever. "Not as yet, Melody. We're looking here, but we don't have much to go on."

"Okay, keep looking," said Melody, shaking her head at Harvey. "We're going to split up, see if we can get into the maintenance areas."

"Splitting up is fine, Melody," said Reg. "But we ran some calculations, and a rucksack full of explosives would need to be fairly close to its target. The further away from the public space, the less effective it will be."

"Yeah, copy that. The stores are all closed. The only things open are the coffee shops, I guess so the store workers can get a coffee before work."

Melody joined Harvey, who was leaning against the handrail of the atrium, looking down at the six floors of shops below.

"Why here?" asked Harvey.

"Why not? It's a public place, lots of damage."

"Yeah but look around. There's nowhere to hide it," replied Harvey.

"Reg said that a rucksack full of explosives would need to be fairly close to its target to be effective. The staff areas behind the scenes would be too far away to do much damage. If the target is the Sheikha, she wouldn't go behind the scenes, I'm guessing."

"So why here?" Harvey asked again.

"Because she's shopping I guess," said Melody.

"And is it usually made public knowledge when somebody like the Sheikha goes shopping?"

Melody thought on what Harvey said. "No, probably not. What are you getting at?"

"I don't know. It just seems odd to me that Crowe knew in advance about a shopping trip."

Melody turned away and closed her eyes, focusing on the issue. The what, why and where didn't add up. As she turned away and took a step, a tiny rush of wind lifted her hair slightly, along with the familiar sound of a bullet rushing past.

"Down," she said and hurled herself to the floor. Harvey ducked down and slid away from the glass handrail.

"Somebody's on to us," she called as she slid herself over to Harvey.

A quick look at the ceiling far behind them told Harvey all he needed to know.

"Three things. He's got a silencer, he's below us, and he's not a cop."

Melody glanced behind them and found the damaged plasterboard ceiling. Gypsum powder still fell lightly from the impact. Harvey chanced raising his head to get an idea of the shooter's position. He saw nothing and no shots were fired.

"He's down there somewhere," said Harvey, "waiting for the perfect shot."

Reg's voice came through, broken and distorted. "You want the good news or the bad news?"

"I'm lying on the floor being shot at," said Melody, "I'll take the bad news. Give me something to look forward to."

There was a short delay. "Sheikha Alia is opening a chain of designer handbag stores, and the one in the mall where you are is apparently the flagship store. It's being opened today at ten am."

"Oh great," replied Melody. "So we can assume the bomb is set to detonate at that time too. What's the good news?"

"There's twenty-five percent off for the first ten customers of the day."

"It's a bad time for jokes, Reg. We've got about three hours to find this bomb and being shot at is not helping."

"Okay, my bad. But what if I told you that there's a long corridor beside a massive electronics store on level six?"

"How did-"

"Jess is on the CCTV system. We can't see the name of the store, the camera is at a funny angle, but we can see movement down there."

"Reg, you're a star," said Melody. Catching Harvey's attention, she explained, "Sixth floor, next to an electronics store. The Sheikha is opening the flagship store of her new designer handbag chain this morning."

"That's why the bomb is here then," said Harvey. "That's how Crowe knew the Sheikha would be here."

"How about I stay up here and keep him occupied, and you

go down and finish him?" said Melody. "There's a fire escape stairwell behind us."

"Saving your backside again, right?" said Harvey.

"You can always stay here and let him shoot at you while I go down and take him out."

"Choices, choices," replied Harvey, as he slid across the tiled floor towards the fire escape.

Melody popped her head up and peered through the glass to try to find the shooter. No shots were fired. She moved along to a large pillar, periodically popping her head up to let the shooter know she was still there.

"Melody," said Reg, "you might have a little problem."

"Go for it, Reg," said Melody. "What on earth could go wrong now?"

"There are two more men heading your way."

CHAPTER THIRTY-EIGHT

Jackson stepped back into the operations room and took a cursory glance around to make sure everyone was working, not because he micromanaged, but because his words to Tenant had to be kept confidential. He touched Reg's shoulder and gestured at the small glass meeting room.

Reg asked Jess to keep an eye on the mall CCTV and alert Melody to the two newcomers' movements. He then followed Jackson to the fishbowl, pulled up a seat, and sat down, interlocking his fingers on the table. "This'll need to be quick, sir," he began. "Melody and Harvey have company, and we're their eyes."

Jackson looked back over his shoulder at Jess, who was flicking from screen to screen.

"Do you have an update for me? Has there been any progress?" asked Jackson calmly.

"We tracked Crowe's movements, where he'd been, where he'd spent the most time, and where a likely target might be."

"And where do you think the target is?" asked Jackson.

"It wasn't easy, sir, and right now, we have no concrete

evidence," said Reg. "But if Crowe wanted to really implicate the UK in a bombing, the target would need to be substantial."

"Agreed," said Jackson.

"One of the places he spent the most time, six hours to be precise, was the mall."

"You think he's going to maim the general public? Get them against us too?"

"No," said Reg, "well, yes, but they'll be collateral. We think he was targeting a Sheikha, the daughter of some Sheik." Reg heard how ridiculous and exaggerated the words sounded when they left his mouth. "I know it sounds far-fetched, sir, but the evidence is stacking up."

"The Sheikha will be in the mall?" asked Jackson. "And how would Crowe have known that?"

"She's opening a chain of stores, designer stuff. This one is the flagship store and she's opening it today. It's in the media, has been for two weeks."

"Okay, good work. So where do you think the bomb is?" asked Jackson.

"The store itself. She'll be right outside."

"In range?"

"Exactly, sir."

"Tenant, I have to tell you something. But it goes no further than this room."

Reg didn't reply. He just raised his eyebrows, waiting for Jackson to deliver the blow.

"I've been to see the old man," said Jackson.

"So far, nobody knows about this, sir. If he's worried about-"

"He's not worried about anything, Tenant. It's me that needs to be worried."

"How come?" asked Reg, leaning forward in his seat. "I don't see how this affects you."

"I've been put in a position, Tenant. I can either get Mills and Stone out of there and hide them away, though God knows they'd be in hiding the rest of their lives..."

"Or?" asked Reg, his brow furrowing.

"Or, we give them up. Let Dubai arrest them, kill them, whatever comes first. Deny all knowledge of them and avert the whole situation."

Reg was stunned. "Give them up? They're-"

"Expendable. It was the plan all along. The old man wanted Stone out of the picture, and he isn't too fussed if Mills goes with him. They're just pawns to him."

"Pawns? I don't see that we have any option, sir," said Reg. "We get them out."

"And the bomb?" asked Jackson.

Right then, Jess stuck her head in the room. "Sorry to interrupt. Reg, we have a problem."

CHAPTER THIRTY-NINE

"Do you want to tell me why I just had the Prime Minister on the phone, asking me why we're monitoring Dubai traffic and private CCTV cameras?"

Jackson pulled his phone from his ear, closed his eyes, took a deep breath then lied.

"We're not, sir. I made it clear that the team were not to use intrusion methods. They know how sensitive the situation is."

"Sounds like somebody didn't understand you, Jackson," said the old man. "Apparently, some Dubai official just issued a formal warning. He told us to cease and desist."

"Cease and desist? What is this, a war?"

"It damn well will be, Jackson, if you don't get your team in line."

The old man hung up, and Jackson stepped out of the fishbowl.

"What's the problem, Tenant?" he asked.

"We got a trace from Dubai. They know we're on their systems. They kicked us off twice, but we found a back door."

"Are you still on there?"

"Officially, sir?"

"Tell me straight, Tenant," said Jackson. "Now is not the time for fluff."

"We got kicked off, so we rerouted the connection to make it look like we're someone else. Hopefully, by the time they figure it out, we'll be out of there."

"Should I ask who we're masquerading as?"

"Probably best not to, sir. Least said, soonest mended, and all that."

Jackson shook his head in disbelief. "You're going to start World War Three, Tenant," he hissed.

"Sir, if we can't see what's going on in the mall, we could lose Melody and Harvey."

"Tenant, if you get caught on their systems, we'll lose a lot more than two bloody operatives."

"Understood, sir," said Reg. "But there's one thing I don't get."

"Go on," said Jackson.

"See the two guys here," Reg pointed to two men dressed in casual clothes. Both men were walking either side of the atrium, closing in on Melody's position.

"Yeah, I see them," said Jackson. "Who are they? Does she know they're coming?"

"I just told her. But, well, sir, there's a third, and he's been shooting at Melody and Harvey."

"Who are they? Do we know yet?"

"They're clearly not local, but they are tanned," said Reg. "Also, we showed Melody a house, right out in the desert. It was where Crowe had been staying."

"So what?" said Jackson, confused as to how the information was relevant.

"She said she'd been there already. It was where she met that Bob guy."

"Bob? The operative?"

"So he *is* an operative then?" asked Reg.

"Officially?" said Jackson.

"I'll take that as a yes, then," said Reg. "You think he's dirty?"

Jackson lowered himself onto one knee to the side of Reg and spoke very quietly. "I think there's a lot more at play here than we know about. Tell me, Tenant, do you trust Jess?" he asked.

Reg's eyes widened. "Of course. She's like a third hand for me right now."

"I need her to do some digging for me."

CHAPTER FORTY

The last thing the sniper felt were Harvey's hands gripping the side of his head and then snatching it to one side. Harvey had run down the fire escape and seen the man lying prone in the narrow alleyway designed as both a fire escape and entrance to the rear of the stores. A door led off from the main alley into an even narrower corridor, painted lime green with six-inch red pipes fixed to the ceiling.

Harvey dragged the body through the door and into the service corridor. He heaved the man into a large plastic bin on wheels and covered him with a few black rubbish bags.

It was as he closed the lid and readied himself to go back out to get Melody that something he'd seen caught up with his racing mind. He turned back and reopened the lid of the bin to confirm exactly what he'd seen. Inside was loose trash, as well as bags of used packaging, the same as any other bin in any other mall. There was a flattened cardboard box, and printed on the side was the word, 'Princess.' Then beside it was, what Harvey guessed to be, the Arabic equivalent in a long swirling font to the right of the English spelling.

He checked the doors either side of the bin. One was the

electronics store, but the other had the sign removed. He tried the door. It was locked. There were no cameras along the corridor so Harvey tested the top and bottom of the door, pushing and feeling for where the locks were. If the door was the main exit, and the actual store was locked from the inside, then it could be the only way in. He gave a shove with his shoulder and felt the door give, but it didn't open. So he stepped back, and with all his strength, kicked out at the door. The heel of his foot slammed into the wood beside the lock and splintered the frame. One more kick and the door popped open and banged against the wall behind.

Harvey checked the ceiling corners for cameras or alarms and saw nothing. He stepped inside.

CHAPTER FORTY-ONE

The warning Reg had given Melody had been timely. As the two men closed in on her, one from either side, she checked around and had no escape except one. Melody was out of sight behind one of six columns that bordered the circular atrium. She watched from her spot on the floor as the two men walked slowly and casually toward her. As soon as they were both behind a column, she quietly got to her feet, pulled herself over the handrail, and lowered herself down, hanging over the seven-floor drop with her fingers barely gripping the smooth tiled floor above.

It seemed like an eternity until the two men met where she had been lying, and spoke in clear English.

"What the-?" said the first man.

"Where did she go?" said the second.

"I didn't see anything," said the first man. "Okay, keep cool. She's got to be around somewhere. Keep your gun holstered unless you have to. The last thing we need is the plod turning up."

"She was just here, Jim," said the second man. "Try the fire exit. I'll stay here and keep an eye out."

Melody's arms began to tremble with her weight. She edged across to get her fingers into a better position and swung her legs toward the column to take some of her weight. The smooth concrete upright had no footholds, but the grip on her boots eased her hands enough to get some strength back.

Pulling up into a chin-up position, she chanced a look back through the glass. The man had his back to her and was just one metre from the handrail. She saw the fire escape door in the distance and knew she had to take the chance. Melody quietly swung her leg up then switched her hands from the tiled floor to the underside of the smooth glass. She waited to make sure the man hadn't heard her then pulled herself up behind him. Holding the glass with one hand, with the other, she slowly removed her belt, made a loop, and quickly slipped it over the man's head, pulling back with all her weight.

The man was caught off guard and slammed into the glass handrail. His neck was pulled back at a horrific angle. Melody kept her weight on the belt. With her free hand, she reached over, grabbed the front of the man's belt and heaved him backwards over the top of the glass.

She watched him fall. His face twisted in fear at his futile attempts to grip something, anything. Less than two seconds later, he was seven floors down with two broken legs, a smashed pelvis, a broken back and a crushed skull. It took three more seconds for him to die.

Melody pulled herself back over the glass handrail and looked down to the sixth floor in time to see the first guy heading towards the sniper, where Harvey would be.

More store employees had begun to file into the mall. It was no longer an empty space, and pretty soon someone would find the body seven floors below. She ran to the fire escape and down the stairs three at a time, then stopped at the door to the sixth floor. Peering through the window, she saw the back of the man on the far side of the mall, heading into the alleyway where the sniper had been. Two shops down from the alleyway, she saw what they had been looking for, a brand new shop with Princess written in glittery font like it had been hand-scrawled. Beside it was the Arabic translation in the same style. The man disappeared through a door to the right, so Melody took her chance.

She bumped into an Asian girl as soon as she stepped into the mall. Apologising, she turned and made her to the alleyway. Her watch said seven forty-five. The shops were all still closed, but the staff were growing in numbers. Various uniforms, various nationalities. As casually as she could, Melody scanned the people, looking for somebody out of place. But she saw no-one.

Reg's voice came loud and clear through her ear-piece. "Melody, are you there?"

"Not a good time, Reg. What's up?"

"Well, if you look up to your right, you'll see the camera I'm looking through, and luckily for you, I saw everything and managed to stop recording."

"Lucky for me, not so lucky for the fella I just threw off the seventh floor."

"It's not all good news, Melody," said Reg, with caution in his voice. "I'd say you have about five seconds to get out of sight."

Melody stopped and turned around instinctively. "Why?"

A scream, loud and piercing, filled the atrium.

CHAPTER FORTY-TWO

There was no need to walk quietly along the narrow service corridor, Melody heard the sounds of the two men fighting before she'd even opened the ruined door. It opened up into the backroom of the Princess store, and the first thing Melody saw was Harvey smashing a fire extinguisher into the man's face.

The shelves that had been neatly fixed to the wall gave way under the man's weight, and he crumpled to the floor.

"We've got about two minutes to get out of here," said Melody.

Harvey stood poised with the extinguisher in his hand and saw the look of urgency on Melody's face.

"What did you do?" he asked.

"Nothing you wouldn't have done," said Melody defensively.

"Just messier, yeah?"

"Kinda," replied Melody.

"I'm not going anywhere until he wakes up and tells me who put him up to it."

Melody looked down at the man on the floor. He was out

cold and his bloodied nose was already swelling. "I'll search the store."

She stepped past Harvey who had bent down to tie the man's shoelaces tightly around his ankles and then together in a firm knot.

Melody worked methodically from left to right, taking down every bag and garment. She first felt for weight and then checked inside. The search took just five minutes and did nothing but prove that the bomb wasn't in the front of the shop.

"Nothing," she called, as she stepped into the back room to find Harvey stood over the man with an aerosol can and lighter in his hand.

"What are you doing?" asked Melody.

Harvey didn't reply.

"Harvey, listen to me, you can't do that."

Harvey tested the spray.

"Squirt him with the fire extinguisher," said Harvey. "Wake him up."

Melody did as instructed. She knew Harvey better than anyone and knew he would go through with it. She slapped the man and sprayed water from the extinguisher over his face until he began to come around.

"Move back," said Harvey.

Melody did as she was told.

Harvey lit the lighter and aimed the spray at the man's face. He gave it a short blast, not enough to injure him, but enough to wake him up quickly. He looked up at Harvey, dazed and confused, then realised he was bound. Harvey gave a test burn into the space beside him.

"Who?" said Harvey.

The man's throat issued a croaky and weak mumble.

Another test burn.

Another feeble murmur.

This time, Harvey didn't hold back. He gave a full second, directly into the man's face. The smell of burning hair and scorched skin instantly filled the small room. Through gritted teeth, the man bucked and rocked, but couldn't move.

"You have five seconds between each burn. If you talk, you earn yourself another five seconds," said Harvey. "Starting now."

"Go fuck yourself."

Harvey lit the lighter and counted down.

He sprayed, and the man rocked back into the wall in agony. But still, he didn't cry out. Instead, he just growled through his teeth.

"Five," said Harvey.

The man was panting, controlling the pain.

"Two."

The man prepared himself for the oncoming pain.

Harvey sprayed.

"Don't make it hard on yourself. You're not scarred yet. Let's start again," said Harvey. "Five. Who's controlling you?"

"Crowe."

"Three," said Harvey. "Crowe's dead, and I'm not stupid. One."

Harvey sprayed.

"I can do this all day," said Harvey, reaching down and pulling the man back upright from where he'd fallen onto his side.

"Who? Five."

"I don't know his name."

"Three," said Harvey. "You get your orders from someone."

"No, I-"

Harvey sprayed.

The smell of burning skin was thick in the air, so Melody closed the door as best she could. The man pulled his knees up as far as they would go and buried his face in his thighs, trying to ease the pain, trying to wipe the hot evaporating liquid from his face.

"Five. Who gives you your orders?"

"I can't say."

"Three."

"No, not again. Okay, okay it's Bob."

"You're learning," said Harvey. "You just earned a bonus round. Who's Bob?"

"I don't know. He's the team lead."

"Is that his real name?"

"No, none of us have real names. I'm Jim."

"Five," said Harvey. "Keep talking."

Jim was fighting for breath. His eyes were closed tight against the pain. "You don't know who we are. If you did, you wouldn't-"

"Wouldn't what?" asked Harvey.

Jim opened his eyes and flinched at how tender they were, but looked up at Harvey, somehow managing to pull a wry grin. "You'd run a mile if you knew."

Harvey sprayed.

"Tell me where the bomb is."

Jim's shave was scorched. The skin on his face had turned an angry red. "I've said too much already. You're going to have to kill me."

"Three," said Harvey.

"No, no more," pleaded Jim.

"One."

"Okay, okay, I'll talk."

"Five. Is the bomb in here?"

Jim shook his head.

"Three. Where did you hide it?"

"*We* didn't hide it."

"Who did? Crowe? He was at the mall all day."

"Do you honestly think he would bring it here himself?"

"So who did?"

Jim didn't reply. He just laughed, a low, painful laugh. His face was too scorched to move his jaw, but from somewhere inside him, a laugh emanated.

"Five."

"You fool."

"Three."

"Don't you see?"

"One."

"You did."

CHAPTER FORTY-THREE

"Sir, I've found something. I think we should go somewhere private," said Jess.

Jackson gave the rest of the room a cursory look and then held the door to the fishbowl open for her. "Reg, are you joining us?" he said.

Jess and Reg sat opposite Jackson, who sat with his hands clasped, ready to listen.

"I did as you asked, sir," said Jess.

"How did you get on?"

"It felt wrong, I feel like a traitor."

"What did you find, Jess?" asked Jackson, ignoring her morality.

She gave Reg a sideways glance, and then spoke clearly, but softly, as if she thought the room was bugged.

"It took some digging, but I managed to go back four weeks," began Jess. "The data is saved incrementally, with the newest data overwriting the oldest each thirtieth day of the new cycle."

Jackson nodded, as if already aware of how the disaster recovery system worked.

"First of all, I looked for patterns in his movements, and

then highlighted the anomalies. He's in here six days a week, plays golf on his day off, and goes to his local pub on the way home from work on a Thursday."

"No deviation?" asked Jackson.

"Not much. He took his wife shopping, but he stayed in the car while she went and shopped."

"What else?"

"I have a friend in facilities, sir," said Jess. "I know it was wrong of me, but I had no choice, I asked him to talk to accounts and get me the phone records."

"Mobile phones? We can get that information here."

"Landlines, sir," said Jess. "His desk phone."

"Are you going anywhere with this?" asked Jackson.

"I managed to get three months of records for his extension. Actually, I got the whole department's. I didn't want it known that I was investigating him."

"Good call. And?" said Jackson.

"Well, sir, I wondered what he does here on Saturdays. We're only in the office if an operation is live, and this is the first major operation we've had for a while."

"Let me guess, he wasn't just catching up on his paperwork?"

"No sir." Jess paused. "He was on the phone to Dubai."

"Anywhere else?"

"No, just Dubai, eight am every Saturday until four weeks ago, when he presumed the data would be overwritten. But the landlines don't work like that."

"Does anybody else know about this?" asked Jackson.

"You said to keep it quiet."

"Good. Here's what we're going to do."

CHAPTER FORTY-FOUR

"My office. Now."

The old man had a way with words, and Jackson's experience had taught him that time was running out. When men with as much power as the old man wanted something, they typically got it.

Jackson disconnected the call, nodded to Reg and Jess, and left the operations room.

He didn't knock on the old man's door, but he did take a breath when he stepped inside and saw the two well-dressed officials standing in front of the old man's desk. They both turned to watch Jackson as he closed the door, reading his movements, looking for guilt.

The old man was sitting back in his chair. His hands were placed on the leather-clad arms, showing his signet ring on one finger and his wedding ring on the other.

"Jackson, this is Mr Marsh and Mr Fowler. Are you aware of who they are?" said the old man.

"Expensive suits, well-tailored, royal crests on your cufflinks, I'd say Downing Street?"

"Close," said Marsh. "We represent the foreign office."

"Are you selling something?" asked Jackson. "I'm very busy, so-"

"Get your team out of Dubai's security systems, Mr Jackson."

Jackson cocked his head. "We're not inside Dubai's security system."

"The debacle with Mr Turvey has caused a plague of viral media. Although Dubai was never mentioned in the incident, the information has come from somewhere, and the talk of the bomb, well, naturally the Dubai Government are keen to get to the bottom of this. So imagine their surprise, Mr Jackson, when they then find an intruder on their satellite systems, monitoring the very mall where Sheikha Alia, who is a very public figure, is opening a store today."

Jackson opened his mouth to talk, but Fowler spoke first.

"We have not come here to *ask* you to get out of Dubai, Mr Jackson. We have come to inform you, personally, that you are no longer operational." Fowler handed over a brown envelope stamped with the official crest. "Following this conversation, you will leave here and inform the rest of your team that they are to go home. They'll be assigned to other duties, details of which will be disclosed once this torrid affair has been dealt with."

"You're shutting us down?" said Jackson.

"Frankly, Mr Jackson, if I were you, I would be grateful that it's Mr Marsh and I standing before you now, and not the foreign minister or the PM himself. Luckily for you, both men are far too busy trying to repair the damage you're causing. Firstly, by operating on foreign soil without instruction. Secondly, by managing an operation so poorly that the entire world saw a live kidnapping of an operative's family and the downright outrageous murder of the perpetrator. And thirdly, by allowing the announcement of a potential bomb to be broadcast to the world. How on earth you thought you would get away with it without us finding out is beyond me. But mark my words, Mr Jackson, your career in British Intelligence is finished."

"Do you have any questions?" asked Marsh.

"No, sir," said Jackson.

"Then we bid you good day, and good luck finding a new career."

The two men left the room, and the old man opened his desk drawer. He placed two glasses on the desk and began to fill them.

"I told you to leave it alone," said the old man.

"You told me to send Mills in the first place," replied Jackson.

"If you had done as I had told you, this would all be over by now."

Jackson sat on the edge of the guest seat. His career sat even more precariously on a knife-edge.

"I pulled the team off before I came up," he lied. "You were right, Stone and Mills are a lost cause. It seems futile now. I guess we'll see what the news has to say about it."

The old man nodded. "So you're coming around," he said. "Finally learned the hard way, did you?" He sat forward and leaned on the desk. His cuff-links knocked heavily on the wood. "Don't fight it. You'll be demoted, but I'll see to it that you don't have to wear a uniform. But you'll still start near the bottom."

"You can do that?" asked Jackson.

"Like I said before, you don't get to sit here without knowing a thing or two, and knowing how to play the game. You're not the first, and you won't be the last, to learn the hard way."

"What about Stone and Mills?" asked Jackson.

"Forget about them. They're history. Right now, they'll either be being arrested or being shot. It's a shame about Mills, she could have been good. I looked at her record. But with a liability like Stone, it was destined for failure."

"And the bomb?"

"Not our problem."

"But it's British made."

"We'll deny it. Stone will take the blame. We'll show Dubai the media footage. Crowe makes it clear he was setting us up. Our ties may be fragile, but there are two hundred years of history that one man can't destroy."

"So that's it then?" said Jackson. "It's all over."

"Turvey will be replaced. It would have been you, but you're out now. So someone else will fill your shoes. This place changes. You have to roll with the punches."

"You'll stay?" asked Jackson.

"I have a year or so left in me. I'll see it out until the end."

"I'll see you before I go," said Jackson. "I'll go give the team the good news."

Jackson stood and made towards the door.

"Jackson," called the old man. Jackson turned and watched the old man relax in his chair like a fat cat that knew he'd get the mouse all along. "Don't be hard on yourself, just learn from it. Morality is a good thing to have, but playing the game is the key."

Jackson closed the door behind him.

CHAPTER FORTY-FIVE

"We need to move, now," said Melody, as two policemen ran past the store front.

Harvey tossed the empty aerosol can on top of Jim and left him writhing on the floor to suffer from his burns. He followed Melody out the door. The pair stopped at the end of the service corridor and peered through the small glass window.

"You heard what he said?" asked Melody.

"It was in the Porsche all along, and we delivered it," said Harvey.

"It wasn't the bomb itself that was traceable back to Britain," said Melody. "It was us who delivered it. It feels like we've been set up."

"Jackson?" asked Harvey.

Melody tried to get Reg on the comms. But all that came back was static. She looked at Harvey, grim-faced.

"We're on our own," she said.

"Let's get the Porsche out of here," said Harvey. "We might just get out of Dubai alive."

"And take it where?"

"I have an idea about that," said Harvey, pushing the door

open. The movement surprised an armed cop who was standing to one side of the frame. Before he could react, Harvey had twisted his arm up behind his back, disarmed him, and landed a forehead into the man's nose. Melody took his radio and used his own cuffs from his belt on his wrists.

They bolted through the fire escape door, checked up and down then ran to the seventh floor. A security guard stood at the top of the second flight of stairs, so Harvey launched an uppercut into the man's groin, and helped him on his way down the concrete stairs. Again, he peered through the small window in the door that led out to the mall.

Harvey glanced back at Melody. His knack for communicating his thoughts without words, something he'd learned from his mentor as a child, came in handy. Melody instantly knew that there were obstructions.

They remained unobserved as they edged around the perimeter wall to the exit, where two armed policemen stood smoking and chatting outside. Melody went through alone and caught their attention.

"Hey, excuse me, guys. There's a man on the floor." She pointed vaguely into the mall. "Help him."

The two men threw their cigarettes on the floor and brushed past her. By the time the first one had seen Harvey standing on the inside of the doors, it was too late for them both. In a matter of seconds, they were disarmed and bound just like their colleague on the floor below. One had a broken nose, and the other had a broken forearm from Melody's over-zealous arm lock.

Harvey drove, while Melody found the house in the desert on her phone's map app. She pulled her seatbelt on as Harvey swung the little sports car onto the ramp as fast as he could. He found the balance of clutch and accelerator, and the Porsche gripped the rough tarmac easily. Finally, they hit the ground floor, bumped over a speed bump, and accelerated out onto the main road.

"How much time do we have?" asked Harvey.

"Until the bomb goes off or until we're shot dead?"

"Bomb," said Harvey.

"Forty-five minutes," replied Melody.

"How far is the house?"

"Fifty-five minutes."

Harvey dropped the clutch and slammed the gear stick down into third as a helicopter flew past in the opposite direction and a line of police cars tore overhead on the elevated section.

They were free of the city in less than ten minutes and joined the tail end of the morning traffic.

CHAPTER FORTY-SIX

Reg, Jess and Jackson walked down the steps of MI6 together. Jackson carried a box containing the items that had decorated his office. Reg and Jess just had their laptop bags.

"I'm sorry it had to come to this, sir," said Reg.

"You don't have to call me sir," said Jackson. "Not anymore anyway." He looked both ways on the street and took a breath. "I just wanted to say that it was nothing you guys did, and I appreciate you trying. I just wish we could have got Mills and Stone out of there. They were good people."

"Don't talk like they're dead," said Reg.

"Well, if they're not dead, they'll be locked up for the fore-seeable," said Jackson. "I tried. We tried, I mean. We did our best."

"I just don't understand it," said Reg. "It was just a quick job for Melody."

"There are forces at play here that go way above our pay grades, Reg."

"Like what?"

"Oh, come on, I can't think about it now," said Jackson. "It's over."

"For you, maybe, but not for them. They're out there still. They may be alive."

"Reg, don't get mixed up in this. It's a dangerous game. Trust me; I just learned the hard way."

"You have no idea what I'm capable of, what I've done," said Reg. "Come on, I can handle the truth, and if you're not going to do anything about it, maybe I will."

"See how far it gets you, Reg. I'll tell you if that's what you really want, but trust me when I say stay away."

Reg stared defiantly at Jackson.

"You're serious about this?"

Reg didn't reply.

Jackson stepped in closer to Reg and Jess and spoke quietly. "Think about this, Reg, who gave the order to get Melody out there? And who is the only one who hasn't been moved from his office?"

Reg's mind clicked into place. Jackson saw the realisation hit home.

"Now think about who's next in line for Turvey's job."

"The old man," said Reg. "The old man set them both up. But why? They saved Turvey's life."

"I told you, don't go there. He's a dangerous man. Keep him on your side, but look for a transfer behind the scenes, both of you. He'll take down anyone who stands in his way. That's all you get from me."

Reg nodded and gave a tight-lipped smile. "Good luck, Jackson."

Jackson stared back. "You know what? I suddenly feel like I can do anything I want."

"So what are you going to do?" asked Jess.

"Live a little," said Jackson. "Live a lot." He gave them a final admiring look. "Goodbye, Reg. Goodbye, Jess."

The two nodded, and Jackson turned to walk away.

"That's not a happy ending," said Jess to Reg as they turned to walk in the opposite direction. "Hey, are you okay?" she asked.

"I'm just thinking about Melody and Harvey. It can't be it. It can't be that cut and dry."

"Can you reach them at all?" asked Jess. "On LUCY?"

"You heard what Jackson said, any attempts to reach them will be deemed as a criminal offence. They'll throw the book at me. How can anyone be so callous, Jess? How can anybody in this day and age get away with doing what the old man did?"

"Power and positioning," said Jess.

"Well, he underestimated Harvey, that's for sure. At least Turvey is alive."

They crossed the main road and stepped up onto the pavement. The sky was already dark, and a light rain had begun to fall. Jess linked her arm through Reg's. She didn't speak, and he didn't pull away, but it felt nice, a semblance of warmth in an otherwise cold world.

"What if we could help Jackson at least?" said Jess.

"How do we help Jackson?" asked Reg. "He's out on his ear already."

"What if we somehow got a message to someone up top, you know?"

"You mean send the foreign minister an email?" said Reg. "What are the chances of him paying that any attention?"

"Maybe. But what if he had no choice but to see what we had to say? And what if what we had to say told a few home truths?"

Reg caught where she was heading with the conversation. "You're talking about-"

"Biblical, Reg," said Jess. "I'm talking about the hardest hack you ever did with the biggest risk you've ever taken. But it'll shake up British intelligence, and clean out a few cobwebs at the same time."

CHAPTER FORTY-SEVEN

Far out in the desert, Harvey stopped the Porsche at the end of a street, five hundred yards from the villa. His arm rested on the open window and the cool desert air washed through the car.

"How do you want to play this?" asked Melody.

"The way I see it, we have three choices," replied Harvey. "Drive the Porsche through the gates, leave it for Bob to find, hopefully in less than ten minutes' time. Option two, drive it through the gates, find Bob, and strap him to the bonnet."

"And option three?" asked Melody.

Suddenly the car rear-view mirror filled with light, and the roar of a heavy pickup truck accelerating towards them filled the quiet street. There wasn't time to move. There wasn't time to get out. Harvey reached across Melody and took hold of the door handle, locking her against the seat.

The truck slammed into the back end of the much smaller sports car, shattering the windows. Harvey slammed the car into reverse, lifted the clutch and pinned the accelerator to the floor. Smoke filled the car as its tyres fought the truck's massive torque. But the little car's weight was no match for the much heavier Ford. Melody leaned out the window and fired two rounds at the driver, but he had an MP5 aimed directly at her. The side of the Porsche was chewed up, the mirror smashed into pieces, and the windscreen shattered into glass pieces that fell around them.

The truck was pushing them towards a wall in an empty piece of land between two abandoned villas. The Porsche left the tarmac and began to slide easily across the sand on the wasteland.

"Option three?" asked Melody, eyeing the wall fifty feet away.

"Do you trust me?" asked Harvey.

"Do I have a choice right now?"

Harvey's legs were almost straight as he put as much weight on the brakes as possible. He was heaving on the handbrake.

"When I let go of the brake, this car is going to fly forward. When that happens, we need to be as far away from this car as possible. How many in the truck?"

"Just one. It's Bob," said Melody.

"Good, he's going to get what's coming to him. On my count, jump from the car and give him everything you've got."

"What?" cried melody. "He has a-"

"Three."

"Harvey."

"Two."

Melody pulled the door handle.

"One," said Harvey.

Harvey opened his own door, pulled his foot from the brake, and instantly felt the speed pick up. Jumping out, he rolled across the ground onto broken bricks, glass and sand then sat up on one knee and emptied the handgun he'd taken from the cop into the truck's cab.

He watched as the realisation dawned on Bob's face, but by then, the Porsche had its own momentum. Both Harvey and

Melody dived for cover as the bumper hit the wall, which folded the car's chassis, designed to absorb an impact. The storage compartment under the bonnet of the little Porsche crumpled, crushing the sports bag hidden inside.

Harvey lay across Melody behind a mound of sand and bricks and waited for the explosion.

Instead, they heard the creak of the old Ford's driver door open.

Harvey raised his head and saw Bob standing by the side of the truck forty-feet away. Bob held the MP5 like a seasoned pro. He hit the magazine eject button and let the empty fall to the floor. Then, like a predator who knows his prey is trapped, he slowly pulled a fresh magazine from his cargo pants.

After the grinding of steel on steel and the screech of brakes, the sound of the magazine being loaded was loud in the empty street.

Then came the sound of heavy boots approaching on the sand and gravel as Bob made his way across the wasteland.

Harvey remained lying across Melody. He was waiting for his opportunity, and his window was getting smaller and smaller with each step Bob took.

He looked over the pile of sand and bricks one last time to see Bob taking aim and froze as Bob raised the gun to his shoulder. Harvey's window of opportunity had gone.

Bob's lip curled in hatred as he lowered his face to the weapon's stock and closed one eye. Harvey ducked back down.

Melody had opened her eyes and stared up at him. Their faces were inches apart.

Neither of them moved. No words were spoken. Harvey nodded a silent goodbye and took three deep breaths. He brought his knees up underneath him, ready to jump up and take the gunman down. He knew he'd be hit, but if Melody could have a chance at running, she could get away.

A small tear rolled out of Melody's eye. She knew what he was about to do.

The cocking lever on Bob's MP5 snatched back, metallic and crisp.

Then the timer on the home-made incendiary device inside the sports holdall in the front of the Porsche hit zero.

CHAPTER FORTY-EIGHT

By the time Harvey and Melody had arrived in central London, Dubai police were announcing the failed bombing at one of their prestigious malls. A successful operation undertaken by Dubai's elite undercover unit was how the media had been told to phrase the incident. The statement was designed to reassure the public that they had been in no danger at any time.

It was around the time of that initial press release that Reg was waiting precisely where he'd been told to wait, on the roof of the MI6 building overlooking the River Thames.

He wore his usual duffel coat, buttoned up to his chin to stop the chilled breeze that rolled off the river from attacking his very core. He was met at exactly ten am, not a minute before, not a minute after, exactly as he was told.

"Thank you for coming, Tenant," said the old man as he walked across the rooftop.

"It's okay, sir," said Reg. "Perhaps next time we could use a meeting room though?"

"What I have to say goes no further," said the old man. "Are you trustworthy, Tenant?"

"I've been on the force for ten years, sir. Nobody has ever doubted my credibility."

"That's what I thought, and I'm glad to hear it." The old man shuffled his feet. "About Jackson," he began, "it's a shame. The man had potential. But, as you know, you don't win the game by doing what's right, you win by doing what you're told." The old man eyed Reg up and down. "Can you do what you're told, Tenant?"

Reg listened intently. He wondered how the lies came out of the old man's mouth so easily.

"Of course, sir," said Reg. "There's no emotion. It's black and white."

"Black and white?" said the old man. "Yes, that's what it is. It's a shame Jackson didn't see things that way."

"He was a good operative, sir. But you did what you had to do."

The old man's face tightened, and his whole demeanour changed.

"Tell me, Tenant, how did you do it?" The old man pulled a handgun from inside his jacket.

Reg's body tensed. He straightened from his lazy slouch to bolt upright. He'd been surrounded by danger for most of his career, but it was the first time a gun had been pointed at him.

"Don't play games with me, Tenant. I'm far better, and my armies are a lot stronger than yours."

"I, I-"

"You nearly ruined me, Tenant, with your meddling. I had a nice visit from the minister of foreign affairs thanks to you."

"Really?" said Reg, collecting himself. "Did you have a nice chat?"

"Your cheap sarcastic wit is as cheap as your childish attempts to bring me down, Tenant. Fortunately for me, I've been playing this game a lot longer than you have, and I know the rules better than anyone."

"There are rules?" said Reg. "Seems like you make them up to suit yourself and it's everyone else that suffers."

"It's the losers who suffer, Tenant," said the old man. "And you just lost. Game over."

The old man gave a hand signal, and suddenly Jess was pushed into view by a masked gunman who stepped up behind her, his gun firmly planted into her temple.

"*Jess*," called Reg. "*No. Leave her out of this.*"

"I thought you said there was no emotion, Tenant? I hear the pair of you are growing close."

"*Let her go.*"

"No," snarled the old man like a spoiled child. "You're the last two loose ends. I thought you were trustworthy but clearly, you're a liability, a risk. Just like the other loser, Jackson."

"You'll never get away with this. What did you expect us to do? Isn't it bad enough you killed Melody and Harvey?"

"*That's* an allegation, Tenant. *I* didn't exactly pull the trigger."

"No, but you left them to die. You might as well have killed them yourself. And *what*, now you're going to cover your tracks? Is that it? We're the last ones left to testify against you."

"I had this conversation with Jackson," said the old man. A British Army Westland Lynx helicopter rose up behind Reg. The down-force flapped at Reg's coat. Its fuselage was painted British Army green, and the pilot nodded at the old man before setting the bird down to rest on the helipad beside them. "I'll tell you what I told him," called the old man over the thunderous noise of the rotors. "It's called minimising risk, and I'm damn good at it."

The pilot of the Lynx kept the blades turning, and the old man stepped up closer to Reg. He gestured with his gun at the masked man who held Jess by her hair in front of him. "He'll take care of you both," said the old man. "Goodbye Tenant."

The old man stepped back towards the helicopter, keeping his gun trained on Reg. Then he climbed up into the rear compartment of the Lynx and motioned for the pilot to get airborne. It was as the blades began to pick up speed and the helicopter began to lift off that the masked gunman on the roof pulled the balaclava off.

A mass of long, dark, naturally curly hair bounced softly onto two strong feminine shoulders. Melody Mills released Jess and smiled up at the old man. The three of them began to wave.

The old man was outraged. As he turned to the pilot and shouted to be taken back down, he caught sight of the man beside him. He hadn't seen him when he'd climbed into the chopper. Harvey Stone sat in the far seat with a SIG Sauer P226 aimed at the stunned old man.

Harvey made a circular motion with his finger pointing upwards, then reached across and disarmed the old man. The pilot gently pulled the collective up, taking the helicopter higher and higher.

"Stop," shouted the old man. "Where are you taking me?"

The pilot didn't respond, so the old man took a headset from where it hung and pulled it on. Harvey sat watching and smiling.

"I said, take me down this instant," said the old man.

The pilot didn't reply.

"Who are you?" asked the old man, ignoring Harvey's weapon.

Harvey didn't reply.

"Will somebody damn well tell me what's going on here?" shouted the old man. Spit flew from his mouth in rage.

The pilot eased off the collective at eighteen thousand feet. The air was too thin at the altitude for the helicopter to hover.

By that time, the old man was panicking, struggling to close the door that Harvey had locked in the open position.

"Somebody tell me what the bloody hell is going on."

The pilot spoke for the first time through the in-flight comms.

"Welcome aboard the flight, sir."

"Who are you? Where's *my* pilot?"

"We hope you enjoyed the ride up, and we apologise for the delay. But rest assured the descent will be much faster."

"Take me down," screamed the old man.

"Oh, you'll be going down shortly," said Harvey. "But first, there's a score to settle."

"Who are you?"

"You don't know my name?" said Harvey. "You left me in the desert to take the rap for a murder and a bombing, and you don't even know what I look like?"

"Stone," said the old man.

"You're worse than I imagined," said Harvey. "Killing people sat at your desk. I could almost respect the men you sent after us. At least they had the courage to stand and fight."

"You don't know the half of it."

"Oh, I know," said Harvey. "We have a mutual friend. He told me all about how you never really wanted Melody in the country, and how she was only sent there so I'd go after her willingly. You didn't have the guts to ask me yourself."

"Yeah, well, the plan worked, didn't it?"

"Nearly," replied Harvey.

"It was a shame about your friend Jackson," said the old man, hoping for a rise from Harvey. "But he never would have made it. He's too weak."

Harvey didn't reply.

"How well exactly do you know him?" asked the old man.

"You know he's the spineless coward who left you there? I gave him a choice, you know?"

"Yeah, he told me about the choice you gave him," said Harvey, "and Reg told me about the choice he made."

"It's their word against mine," spat the old man. "Take me down. This is a joke."

"And what about Turvey? You didn't really give him much of a choice, did you? Die or watch his family be killed?"

"Turvey was in the way," snarled the old man. "I knew he would never let his family die."

"In your way?" said Harvey. "You wanted his desk, his job. Is that all this was about? But to get there, you were willing to kill innocent people? You make me sick."

"You don't know the rules of the game," said the old man. "I do. I saw the bigger picture."

"I don't care about *your* bigger picture. It's *my* turn to give *you* a choice, old man," said Harvey.

"Is that right? Just because you're holding a gun, you think you can manipulate me? You have *no idea* who you are dealing with, you impetuous-"

Harvey leaned forward and tossed the gun out the open side door. The weapon span away through the air and disappeared from view.

"What was you saying?" said Harvey. "I don't need a gun. I'll kill you with my bare hands."

"So what?" asked the old man. "What now?"

"Option one," began Harvey, "you jump."

The old man looked nervously out the open door. At eighteen thousand feet, London appeared extremely small.

"Or?" he asked, holding onto the back of the seat and the large u-shaped handle beside the door.

"Or you die an extremely painful and slow death." Harvey

leaned closer to the old man. "And when it comes to slow deaths..." He grinned. "I wrote the book on it."

"Pilot, this is nonsense. Take me down at once. How do I call ATC from here?"

The pilot looked behind him and tapped the cushioned headset that covered his ear.

"*Who are you?*" demanded the old man.

That was when Jackson turned in his seat, raised the visor on his helmet, removed his sunglasses, and winked at the old man.

CHAPTER FORTY-NINE

Jackson brought the helicopter down in a small paddock which sat beside a disused barn near the town of Epping in Essex. Harvey knew it was disused. The area had been his old stomping ground. It was where he had honed his skills under the watchful eye of his mentor, Julios.

"Out," said Harvey to the old man.

The old man looked terrified. He clung to the handrail beside the door of the Lynx and wept.

Harvey stepped past him and jumped to the ground as the rotors slowed to a stop above him. A car sat thirty feet away. Its single occupant had been waiting for them to arrive.

Jackson joined Harvey as he unlocked the old barn, and they began to prepare.

The man in the car waited, controlling his temper and keeping hold of his emotions.

The old man sat in the chopper sobbing to himself.

Harvey pushed the big doors to the barn open to let the light in and the roosting pigeons out. The space was empty, save for the wooden beams that formed the roof truss and a workbench that ran along one side of the room.

In the far corner was a pile of old farm tools, a tractor wheel and other items, with a tarpaulin stretched across to keep the weather from getting to them.

"What first?" said Jackson.

"We need a hole in the ground, three feet square," said Harvey. "There're some shovels under the tarp. Have the old man dig it, it'll keep him busy."

Jackson did as instructed. He pulled a shovel from the corner of the room and strode outside to face the old man, who looked up as Jackson approached with disdain in his eyes.

"It's time to get out," said Jackson, without a quiver of hesitation, emotion or sorrow in his voice.

"What are you going to do to me?" said the old man, eyeing the shovel in Jackson's hands.

Jackson said nothing. He handed the old man the old, heavy shovel, and pointed to a spot in the centre of the paddock. "Dig."

"My own grave? Is that it? You're going to kill me and bury me here, wherever we are."

Harvey stepped out of the barn, looked up into the sky, and then leaned on the barn door. "Not very imaginative, are you?" he said to the old man.

"What do you mean?"

"I thought you would have credited me with a bit more creativity," replied Harvey. "But we're not here to discuss it. You'll find out soon enough. Now go dig the hole."

The old man opened his mouth to say something, but the look on Harvey's face changed his mind. He held the shovel with both hands and took a slow walk to the middle of the small paddock.

"Just there's fine," called Harvey.

The old man stopped, removed his long overcoat, which he

folded and placed on the ground, and then slowly set about digging.

"What do you have planned, Harvey?" said Jackson, once the old man was out of earshot.

Harvey didn't answer the question. "We need firewood and lots of it."

CHAPTER FIFTY

Before long, the old man was waist deep in a grave-shaped hole. Harvey and Jackson had spent two hours gathering the wood while the man in the car had sat and watched. A pile of broken branches, old pallets and dead trees stood six feet high to one side of the hole. Harvey carried a sledgehammer, a long iron stake and a length of rope to the scene and dropped them to the ground.

"What's that for?" asked the old man, leaning on the shovel from deep inside the hole.

Harvey didn't reply.

He hammered the stake into the soft ground a few feet from the hole and fastened one end of the twenty-foot rope to the eyelet at the top end of the stake.

"What are you doing?" asked the old man, becoming very scared. "Tell me. What are you going to do?"

"You ask too many questions," said Harvey.

"I thought you would just shoot me and be done with it. But, but this all seems so dramatic."

Harvey swung the sledgehammer over his shoulder and looked down into the hole. "You earned this. You deserve far more than a quick bullet in the head, and I'm known for making sure people get what they deserve. So shut up and get out of the hole. It's deep enough."

The old man half rolled and half climbed out of the hole on the far side, away from Harvey, the stake and the rope.

Harvey gave him a look.

The old man took a deep breath and gingerly stepped around to where Harvey stood.

"Strip," said Harvey.

"Strip?"

"Strip," Harvey repeated, his diction clear, leaving no room for the old man to question him. The old man removed his clothes and folded them neatly in a pile beside him. He stood with his hands over his genitals and held back his tears.

"Hands," said Harvey.

"Hands?" said the old man. His voice had changed from his authoritative grumble to the high-pitched song of a child.

"Hold them out."

The old man held his hands out for Harvey to begin tying them together. Harvey bound the old man's wrists in a neat series of loops and then wound the rope around his ankles. He completed the binding with a sturdy knot which was neat, with barely any excess rope.

"You've done this before,' said Jackson.

Harvey didn't reply.

"It's cold," said the old man.

"You want us to light a fire?" said Harvey. He began to pull wood into the hole that the old man had dug and then turned to Jackson. "Let's build a fire."

In the distance, the car sat with its engine running to keep the man warm. Before long, the driver saw that the time was approaching, and wiped the tears from his face.

Harvey waited for the fire to get going. He stood motionless, his arms folded across his chest. He stared at the old man.

"I've killed many people," said Harvey. "They all deserved it in one way or another, some more than others. But none of them were mindless murders."

"Is this a confession?" said the old man.

Harvey ignored the old man's comment and continued, while Jackson stood and listened, oddly in awe of Harvey's presence.

"Over the years, I've done some very bad things to some very bad people," said Harvey. "I've learned a thing or two about death and how it works."

Harvey began to walk in a tight circle around the old man, who followed Harvey with his eyes. But when Harvey disappeared behind him, he closed his eyes tightly, too frightened to move.

"There are a series of emotions that most men go through," said Harvey, "when they know death is coming. It's almost like some deep psychology that's ingrained in all of us. Firstly, there's the denial, the anger. Do you remember how you insulted us on the ride here, old man?"

The old man didn't respond.

Harvey stepped up directly behind the old man and whispered into his ear. "Then comes the fear."

The flab on the old man's stomach wobbled as his entire body shuddered.

"The fear brings the tears and the shame, as the human mind spins all sorts of horrific scenarios to a vivid imagining. That's where you are now."

Harvey walked around the front and stood between the old man and the fire.

"You're going to die a very slow and painful death. But know this, old man," said Harvey in his chilled, emotionless tone, "you'll suffer far beyond that which your imagination can conjure up. So whatever you think we're going to do to you, cast the image aside, because it's not even close."

The man's face was shining with tears, and snot ran freely across his wide double chin. Then, with the finality of death itself, he broke. Loud sobs came from deep inside his gut. His body shook with adrenaline and the cold, and urine began to stream down his inner leg.

Harvey glanced across at Jackson, who stood wide-eyed at the way Harvey had broken the man he'd once looked up to, just with words.

Harvey gestured with his head for Jackson to follow him to the barn, and as they stepped inside, Jackson caught Harvey by the arm. "Hey, Harvey," he began, and then removed his hand, "listen. I don't know what you have planned, but are you sure you want to go ahead with this?"

"I'm not going through with anything," said Harvey. "I'm just facilitating, helping a friend."

Jackson looked solemnly back at Harvey's cold eyes and nodded.

"Help me with this," said Harvey, and he pulled back the tarp from the corner of the barn.

CHAPTER FIFTY-ONE

Melody, Reg and Jess walked down the steps of the Secret Intelligence Service building on London's Southbank. They turned right and followed the road around to walk across Vauxhall Bridge. The slight rain had eased off, but a bitter wind blew off the river and bit into their faces.

They were halfway across the bridge when Reg stopped and leaned on the handrail. He looked down into the murky water below then turned to Melody and said what they were all thinking. "Why don't you come work with us, Melody?"

Melody gave a laugh. "I don't think so, Reg," she said. "I've hardly had a break these past few days."

"How about an office-based job?" said Reg. "You'd still be awesome at it."

"Can you honestly see me stuck inside an office for the rest of my life?" replied Melody. "It would drive me insane."

"So, what? You're going to sit in Harvey's farm for the rest of your life?" said Reg. "And do what?"

Melody smiled. "It's such a beautiful place, Reg. We walk to the beach, through the forests and across fields. We eat at stunning French cafes and quaint little restaurants. It's so different from, well here, and don't get me wrong, I love London, but there's something about the green, the quiet and the ocean that just sets your mind at ease. I love it there, Reg."

Reg smiled. The three of them stood side by side leaning on the railing, watching the water flow past beneath them.

"Sounds idyllic, Melody," said Reg. "But don't you get bored?"

"Not bored, Reg," said Melody. "Just..."

"You miss it all, don't you?" said Reg.

"It's complicated," said Melody,

"Reg, don't press her," said Jess. "If she wanted to come back, she would."

Melody looked up at them both then gazed across at the rest of the city.

"It's Harvey, isn't it?" said Reg. "You feel like you have to make a choice."

"Reg," said Jess, "leave her alone."

"It's okay, thanks, Jess," said Melody. "He's right. At least, he's kind of right." Melody put her hands in her jacket pockets and turned to lean her back on the railing. "When Gordon came to find us, and when I had to decide if I was going to come, we had the chat. He doesn't want to hold me back. So it's not him that's holding me, it's me that holding me. Does that make sense?"

"That makes perfect sense to me, Melody," said Jess. "But can I ask you something?"

"Sure, I'm in the spotlight now, might as well get it all out," said Melody.

"I'm sorry, but I have to ask, and I'm sorry if it comes out wrong, but well, it seems to me that Harvey is..."

Jess hung on her last word, searching for the right way to describe Harvey without insulting Melody or Harvey himself.

"Different?" suggested Melody.

"Yes, different," said Jess. "And honestly, I don't mean that negatively, but, well, I've heard the stories, and, if they're all true, then-"

"The stories are all true," said Reg. "But things done in the past don't make him a bad man. In fact, as shocking as some of the stories are, there's honour inside him. He's a good guy."

"Yeah," said Melody. "He has his moral compass that guides him, and he's not as hard as you think. There's a soft side to him."

Reg raised an eyebrow. "A soft side, yeah?"

"Yeah," continued Melody. "I know it's hard to believe. But he makes me coffee in bed, and you should see him with Boon."

"Boon?" asked Jess.

"Boon is their dog," said Reg. "Harvey rescued him when his owner was killed by-"

"I think that's a story for another occasion, Reg," said Melody. "But you'd have to see it to believe it. Harvey is genuinely a sweetheart. He'd do anything for me, and he'll always be the first one to stand up to a bully. I think that's one of his most endearing qualities."

"So this new soft Harvey you met," said Reg, smiling, "what do you reckon he's doing to the old man right now?"

"I don't know, Reg," said Melody. "But I'm sure whatever it is, his moral compass is guiding him." She flashed Reg a smile and turned back around to watch the water flow past.

CHAPTER FIFTY-TWO

The team were all sat in the operations room on Monday morning. Reg was beside Jess, and they'd enjoyed a weekend together, grateful to be alive, grateful to have jobs, and happy that Melody and Harvey had escaped Dubai.

Ladyluck, Gordon and the others were all at their desks, awaiting the briefing that was usually the starting gun for the week. Two people entered the room, a man and woman, both well-dressed and well-groomed. They stood at the far end of the room beside the glass walls of the fishbowl with their hands folded in front of them.

"People, heads up," said the man. "My name is Mr Thorn, and this is Miss Finch. We're sorry to interrupt your morning. I'm sure you're all aware that there have been some changes around here, and we'd like to thank you for your patience. The past week has been a trying time for us all. But we're pleased to say that we're through it, and well, in short, that's entirely down to the professionalism and aptitude that this team demonstrated. And, believe me, it has not gone unnoticed."

The team shared confused glances but smiled at the praise.

"I'll leave the details of Mr Fox and Mr Turvey out of this, and we would appreciate it if you could all treat the entire incident as confidential. If you're approached by journalists, say nothing."

Mr Thorn eyed the room and saw nothing but courteous nods from the men and women who all sat attentively listening.

"We'd also like to introduce you to your new head," continued Thorn. "But before we introduce you, I'd like to say that the gentleman in question has risen through the ranks, and showed the exact attitude and traits that we look for in all our staff. I have no doubt that he will lead you to success. The door opened once more and Jackson stood in the door frame. He hadn't taken a step when everyone in the room stood and applauded him.

The man in the suit cut the clapping short, and the team sat back in their seats.

"Mr Jackson will be seated in the vacant office upstairs and, if anything, you should take note and use him as an example of what hard work and determination will get you."

Reg stepped forward and shook Jackson's hand. "Pleased to have you back, sir."

"I believe it's you I have to thank for that, Tenant," said Jackson. "And, of course, you Jess."

Jess beamed at the recognition, and, as was her habit when she was the centre of attention, she began to clean her glasses with her shirt.

Reg returned to his seat as Miss Finch, who stood beside Jackson addressed the room. "That does, of course, leave a hole in the operations room, and quite frankly, Mr Jackson leaves behind some very big shoes for someone to fill. But after careful consideration, which may have been swayed by the sheer courage this man displayed during recent events, along with his ability to remain focused and calm under severe pressure, we have decided to award the role to Mr Tenant. If he'll take it, of course." She turned to face Reg and smiled a warm but professional smile.

Reg was taken aback and stared disbelievingly at Jess, who held her hands to her face with joy and leaned forward to hug him. A few seconds later, Reg stood, shook the hands of the man, woman and Jackson then returned to his seat.

"Well?" said the smartly dressed man. "Do you want the role or not?"

Reg, ever the introvert, laughed at the sudden attention. "Of course I want the role. But I do have a few conditions."

CHAPTER FIFTY-THREE

The beach and the small village in Argeles-Sur-Mer hadn't changed in the few days that Harvey and Melody had been away.

In the morning, they drank coffee and breakfasted in the small cafe where Gordon had been waiting for them. While they waited, Harvey had pulled the only British paper from the pile of newspapers by the door and flicked through the news, uninterested in any of it.

Melody had skimmed through the paper herself. There was an article about how the Dubai government had averted a near crisis when their special armed response unit had carried out the controlled explosion of a car bomb in a rural street out of town. She flicked past the story. However, she was interested in one particular article about a man who had been found tarred and feathered and been dumped on the high street of Epping town centre. The man was named Augustus Fox and had recently been shamed from a senior role in the British government. Fox, who was still alive but severely burned, faces life imprisonment and extradition to the United Arab Emirates. The story continued to describe how the British have not extradited anybody to the Arab nation since 2011, due to possible torture practices. But, considering the levity of the crimes, and in an effort to maintain peaceful relations with the Emiratis, the Crown Prosecution would be pushing for the extradition ban to be lifted.

Melody peered over the top of the paper at Harvey, who stared back stony-faced. She turned her attention back to the newspaper, deciding not to bring the story up. It was nice to be home. Normality was a long way off, and a lengthy discussion about Harvey's idea of acceptable levels of punishment could be saved for another time.

Boon had been pleased to see them when they'd collected him from their neighbour's place. Although the neighbours had pushed for details of their trip, they had managed to avoid going into too much depth. Melody had bought them flowers and chocolates as a gift and had been forced to accept the invitation to dinner.

As they walked along the beach, Boon ran full pelt along the sand, as if showing off in front of Melody and Harvey, reminding them of how fast he could run. Melody took Harvey's hand in hers and held her flip-flops in her other hand. She loved the feeling of the soft sand beneath her feet.

"About what you said," she began.

"When?" replied Harvey.

"In the car, the Porsche, you told me you'd never felt this way before. Is that true?"

Harvey didn't reply.

"Come on, you were doing well in Dubai, really letting go."

"What do you want me to say, Melody?" said Harvey.

"The truth, Harvey. Where do we stand?"

"I told you how I feel. I don't have to say it over and over, do I?"

"No."

"Well, what then?" said Harvey. "I flew to Dubai to bring you home, and now you're home, I'd like to get back to the way things were."

"The way things were?" Melody said. "And how were things, in your mind?"

"You know, the normal stuff. Morning coffee, training, working on the house," said Harvey. "You wanted to grow some vegetables, right? Well, let's do that." Harvey paused and thought about what he was asking of her. "Unless you still want-"

"No, Harvey, you just said it."

"So you don't want to go back to work?"

"Part of me does, I can't lie," said Melody. "But all of me wants to be here with you."

Harvey began a slow walk and Melody walked beside him, scooping up damp cold sand in her feet with each step.

"You really want to go back?" asked Harvey.

"I just said, I'd rather-"

"But part of you does? Because it's fine, we just have to absorb it."

"Absorb it?" asked Melody.

"Yeah, we have to flex. You know, it doesn't have to be all or nothing."

"So if I worked the odd job, you'd be totally okay with it?"

"Yeah, I guess so," said Harvey. "I did a fair amount of thinking when you left and when I was on the plane, and then again when I was sat on the balcony while you were set up for the shot."

"You what?" said Melody. "You were outside? Four feet from me?"

"The whole time," said Harvey. "I could even smell your shampoo."

"I was there for hours and you didn't think to let me know you were there?"

"I didn't want you to lose focus."

"I have to say," said Melody, "that was a great shot you made from the villa."

"Had a good teacher, didn't I?" replied Harvey. "I'd do it again, you know?"

"Do what?"

"Come and get you, you know, if you were in trouble."

"Yeah, I know. It's nice to know too." Melody opened her mouth and let the words slip away.

"Would it help if we were married?" asked Harvey.

"You what?" replied Melody.

"You know, us. Would it help if we were married? Would it feel more stable for you? To know that you had someone to come home to and to know I'd be there waiting?"

Melody stopped dead in her tracks. "Is that a proposal, Mr Stone?"

Harvey stopped and stared back at her. "Yes. Yes, it is."

Melody laughed and put her hands up to her face. She peeked through her fingers. "You're serious?" she said.

Harvey didn't reply.

"Yes, I'll marry you, Harvey. But you don't get away with it that easily."

"What do you mean?" asked Harvey.

"I want a proper proposal. You're going to have to get romantic on me, Mr Stone," said Melody as she walked past Harvey, who watched her walk, shook his head then followed behind.

Being married didn't scare Harvey, and Melody *had* changed his life. She'd even taught him a few things too. He felt good. He felt like normality was coming. They laughed as they made their way to the lane that led to their little farmhouse. But the laughter came to a stop when Harvey saw the car waiting for them on the road.

It was a black saloon, parked where the lane met the beach road. One man stood to the rear of the car with his hands inside the pockets of his long overcoat.

Boon saw the man and issued a low growl. He looked up at Harvey, waiting for his command.

Harvey stopped ten feet in front of him; Melody stood alongside him. They both stared the dark-haired man up and down. They both noted his crooked nose and cleft lip, and both observed the bulge in his pocket from his sidearm.

"You're a hard pair to find," said the man, as he lit a cigarette and slid a shiny lighter back into the inside pocket of his suit jacket.

"How would you like to come and work for me?"

Harvey didn't reply.

The End

Also by J.D. Weston

Award-winning author and creator of Harvey Stone and Frankie Black, J.D.Weston was born in London, England, and after more than a decade in the Middle East, now enjoys a tranquil life in Lincolnshire with his wife.

The Harvey Stone series is the prequel series set ten years before The Stone Cold Thriller series.

With more than twenty novels to J.D. Weston's name, the Harvey Stone series is the result of many years of storytelling, and is his finest work to date. You can find more about J.D. Weston at www.jdweston.com.

Turn the page to see his other books.

THE HARVEY STONE SERIES

Free Novella

The game is death. The winners takes all...

See www.jdweston.com for details.

The Silent Man

To find the killer, he must lose his mind...

See www.jdweston.com for details.

The Spider's Web

To catch the killer, he must become the fly...

See www.jdweston.com for details.

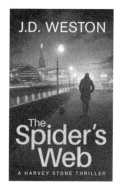

The Mercy Kill

To light the way, he must burn his past...

See www.jdweston.com for details.

The Savage Few

Coming 2021

Join the J.D. Weston Reader Group to stay up to date on new releases, receive discounts, and get three free eBooks.

See www.jdweston.com for details.

THE STONE COLD THRILLER SERIES

The Stone Cold Thriller Series

Stone Cold

Stone Fury

Stone Fall

Stone Rage

Stone Free

Stone Rush

Stone Game

Stone Raid

Stone Deep

Stone Fist

Stone Army

Stone Face

The Stone Cold Box Sets

Boxset One

Boxset Two

Boxset Three

Boxset Four

Visit www.jdweston.com for details.

THE FRANKIE BLACK FILES

The Frankie Black Files

Visit www.jdweston.com for details.

A NOTE FROM THE AUTHOR

Stone Free was the first time I had taken Harvey away from London for an adventure, and where better to take him than my home city of Dubai.

I like to leave a titbit like this for you all at the end of each book. In previous books I explained where certain locations from childhood slot into the Stone Cold Thriller series.

Stone Free is no different.

In 2016, after living in Dubai for close to ten years, I arranged for my family to come out for a visit and as a surprise for my brother's 40th birthday. If you remember that villa on the Palm Jumeirah? Yeah, we rented that out for two weeks and although it was in my home city, with my family there, it was the best holiday I've ever had.

I'll continue to use locations I know in my stories, and I'll continue to explain their significance in these notes. I hope you'll continue with the series. There's so much more to come.

Thank you for reading.

J.D.Weston

To learn more about J.D.Weston
www.jdweston.com
john@jdweston.com

ACKNOWLEDGMENTS

Authors are often portrayed as having very lonely work lives. There breeds a stereotypical image of reclusive authors talking only to their cat or dog and their editor, and living off cereal and brandy.

I beg to differ.

There is absolutely no way on the planet that this book could have been created to the standard it is without the help and support of Erica Weston, Paul Weston, Danny Maguire, and Heather Draper. All of whom offered vital feedback during various drafts and supported me while I locked myself away and spoke to my imaginary dog, ate cereal and drank brandy.

The book was painstakingly edited by Ceri Savage, who continues to sit with me on Skype every week as we flesh out the series, and also throws in some amazing ideas.

To those named above, I am truly grateful.

J.D.Weston.

CPSIA information can be obtained
at www.ICGtesting.com
Printed in the USA
BVHW031756281220
596587BV00005B/20

9 781914 270130